NOMAD, NOMAD
Stories

Advanced Reader's Edition | On Sale June 2021

Advanced Praise for *Nomad, Nomad: Stories*

"Set in Mongolia where there is "more in the sky than in the earth," this collection of stories by Jonan Pilet depicts the raw ferocity of life as a missionary on the steppes. In this book, faith in God and human relationships are tested: plagues of locusts, frozen rivers to cross by horse, and the cold rhythm of long winters brightened by the comfort of a stove's heat and mutton soup. *Nomad, Nomad* is a wonderful debut."

— Karen An-hwei Lee, author of *The Maze of Transparencies*

"In *Nomad, Nomad,* Jonan Pilet joins a distinguished roster of writers whose stories of foreign worlds transcend travel and enter the realm of imaginative quests, of lives and worlds hidden, discovered, and transformed. Pilet's fiction is beautifully wrought and unsparing, tender, revelatory, and wise."

— Robert Clark, Edgar Award-winning author of *Mr. White's Confession: A Novel*

"In prose that is both nimble and vivid, Pilet reveals the cold-lashed, wind-swept exterior landscapes of Mongolia as well as the aching interior landscapes of the rich varied characters traversing these stories. Whereas some writers write as spectators piling up observations, these stories have the feel of lived experience, of a writer writing from the inside out. Each story bristles with tension and astonishing detail. Each story is written with boundless compassion. In each story, Pilet takes our human urges, fears and longings and makes sheer music."

— Gina Ochsner, author of *The Hidden Letters of Velta B.*

"Jonan Pilet's stories are visceral, transporting, and tenderly human— with the lyricism of a poet, he brings his characters and landscapes so vividly to life. I would follow this writer anywhere."

— Danya Kukafka, author of *Girl in Snow*

Nomad, Nomad

Stories

JONAN PILET

Nomad, Nomad

Copyright © 2021 Jonan Pilet

All rights reserved. Published by Bound to Brew, a registered DBA of Team Publishing LLC

Bound to Brew | Team Publishing LLC

9457 S University Blvd. 819 Highlands Ranch, CO 80126

www.boundtobrew.com

This is a work of fiction. Names, characters, businesses, events, and incidents are the products of the author's imagination. Any resemblance to actual persons, living or dead, or actual events is purely coincidental.

Library of Congress Cataloging-in-Publication Data (pending)

ISBN 13: 978-1-953500-10-6 (trade paperback)

ISBN 13: 978-1-953500-11-3 (ebook)

Edited by Pauline Harris & Typeset by Nicole Zamudio-Roman

Subscription Box Edition Book Cover designed by Reagann Larson

First Edition: June 2021

Printed in the United States of America

10 9 8 7 6 5 4 3 2 1

To my family, friends, and everyone who has made a home for this nomad —

Contents

Sewer Dogs

The dirt kept Od's gender hidden, and the other boys living with her in the sewers of Ulaanbaatar's fourth district didn't give her secret away. When she first arrived, one of the older boys, Gan, cut her hair so she would look like the others. She knew, and was told, that eventually when she was older, she would have to leave. Someone would find and take her, they'd clean and dress her, and then sell her. Some of the boys said it would be better because she'd live in a house and always have plenty to eat.

"Die!" they yelled. "Die!" A group of boys dressed in school uniforms trapped a puppy in a corner. They took turns kicking it. Od was looking through the dumpster outside an apartment across the street. She stood on Gan's shoulder to climb up and inside the bin. When she found a Fanta bottle with a bit of orange liquid left, she took a sip and tossed the rest down to Gan. When she found a partially eaten chocolate rice bar, she took a bite, but left most for Gan, who licked the wrapper clean. They would look longer, for something more, but it was too cold to spend more than a few minutes above the surface in their ragged coats and torn pants. She called for Gan and he helped her down.

The schoolboys were still kicking the dog as Gan and Od passed. Od stopped and waited, watching them, but was noticed by one of the boys. He turned and tossed a stone at her. "Dog," he yelled. The stone skipped off the concrete and nicked her leg, drawing blood. Gan pulled on her arm and dragged her away before any of the other boys' attention was pulled away from the puppy. Once around the corner, Od yanked her arm away and peered around the edge of the building to see the boys, still beating the dog. The whimpers traveled over the empty playground and echoed off half-circle of concrete apartment buildings.

Gan tugged on Od's ear to get her attention and tried to get her to leave as he shook from the cold. "Come on," he said. "We're going to freeze."

Od's knees smacked together as she pushed Gan away. He cursed and ran to the nearest manhole. He pushed the cover out of the way and climbed down, covering it back up behind him.

A group of schoolgirls walked past the boys and they forgot about the dog, instead they chased the girls, hollering at them, making them scream and laugh.

Od snuck back around the corner and over to the dog. No longer whimpering, it didn't move. It remained curled

in a ball, blood dripping from its mouth. Od picked up
one of its chipped white teeth and rolled it in her shaking
fingers. She bent down and placed her hand on the dog's
head, and then its chest. It was warm, its heart was beating, and it shivered slightly. It grunted as she scooped it
up in her arms, its blood smearing on her coat. One of
its eyes was swollen shut, but the other looked up at her.

"You have stars in your eye," she said. It was the same
thing her mother had told her. One of the few things she
remembered about her life before the sewers.

"You have stars in your eyes," her mother had said as
they stood on top of a hill outside the city. To Od, this
hill was a mountain, and the stars weren't just above.
They were everywhere, touching everything. Od and her
mother left her father on that hill. They didn't bury him.
Instead, they left him there to join the stars, and let the
wind carry him, up and away. "Your dad must have put
them in your eyes, so he'd always be with you."

Od ran with the puppy as one of the boys came back
and yelled, "Drop it!"

She rounded the corner, and with her free hand, pushed
up the manhole cover and climbed in. She closed it before
the boy caught up and listened to the other boys as they
arrived at the cover; they stood above and blamed each
other for losing the dog. They wouldn't follow her down
here, especially not in their school clothes. She cradled
the puppy as she climbed down the rusted ladder. She
had to keep the puppy hidden. If any of the others saw
it, they would take it and eat it. Only Gan wouldn't take
it, and that was because Od would beg him not to. But

even Gan wouldn't stop the other boys from taking it; he owed those boys his life, just like Od owed hers to Gan.

Gan had found her after her mom had died. When her mother got sick, she told her to go into the city, and find her uncle, that he would take care of her and keep her as his own. Od spent days on the streets and in the cold and couldn't find him. She pulled on strangers' arms, asking if they were "*Chuluun,*" telling them "*Bayar*, mother," sent her. Od spent her last night alone, tucked in a corner between two apartments. It smelled of urine, but it was out of the wind. She lay there as the cold moved in and stilled her. It was comforting, and she was happy. She saw her father and his horse. He lifted her onto it and squeezed her hand. He led the horse and called Od a mighty warrior, *daichin khun*. Her mother joined them and yelled at him because the skin between Od's boots and pants was showing. "Too cold," she said, taking Od off the horse and tucking her pants into her boots.

Od fell asleep warm, ready to join her parents, wherever they were, thinking maybe she already had. But when she woke, she was in terrible pain. Blood rushed into her legs, arms, fingers, and toes, spreading fire through her limbs. Gan had found her and saved her by carrying her into the sewers. He soothed her as she screamed, and took her hands between his and rubbed them, and then rubbed her feet back to life, telling her it would get better. Gan told Od his parents were gone too, and that the kids in the sewers were a new family, a family that would look out for her, and together they would make sure they always had food to eat.

"Quiet," she told the whimpering dog. "You have to stay quiet." She waited at the bottom of the ladder for her eyes to adjust to the dark, then moved down the sewer corridor. There were clean sewers with dry floors, heated by piping, but those sections were claimed by men, older, larger, and stronger than the children. They were men who worked during the day and spent all they had on vodka for the night. If the children went near those sections, they'd have empty bottles hurled at them. If they were caught, they'd be beaten and sent away as a warning to the others. So, the children kept warm in the tunnels where sewage leaked from pipes and left a constant puddle of human waste and bath water from the apartments above. But, the radiator pipes pinned to the comment walls, too hot to touch, thawed and warmed everything inside.

It hadn't taken Od long to get used to the smell. And after a year of living in the sewer, she barely noticed it anymore. Gan was waiting for her further down the passage and cursed at her when he saw the dog. "Not dinner," he said.

"Not dinner," Od repeated.

Gan held up a rat he had caught, and together with the living dog and the recently dead rat, they moved further in and to their bed — a collection of bricks, placed together to make a platform, raised slightly higher than the sewage, and on top of that a mound of plastic and fabrics for warmth.

Od sat on the platform with Gan and the puppy. He dismantled the rat, removing its head and tail. Peeling back its fur, he said, "You'll have to keep it hidden."

"I know," Od answered.

"You think it will live?" Gan asked, ripping a leg from the rat and handing it to Od.

"If it eats," she said. She held the leg to the puppy and said, "Please." The puppy had its one eye open, and its nose twitched as the rat leg came near. Od tore the flesh off the small bone and stuck it into the dog's mouth. It pushed the food out with its tongue, but Od pushed it back in. "You must eat," she said. She pushed her finger down the dog's throat, making it swallow the rat meat.

"*You* must eat," Gan said, handing her a bloody strip of flesh from the rat's side.

Od tore the piece in two, ate one, and forced the other down the dog's throat again. She took the water bottle they shared: they knew which stores to visit and when to visit them to get their bottles filled. Gan finished the rat and set the inedible parts, bones, intestines, and skull, in a plastic bucket, hoping to attract more rats. Od laid down next to the dog, holding it close to keep it warm and make it feel safe. She closed her eyes and tried to remember her mother's lullaby.

"*Like the chick of the white duck,*" Od sang, "*I call my mother from far away.*"

When her mother died, Od tried to take her body to the mountain. But she wasn't strong enough. She couldn't even get it outside the *ger*— their small round home.

"Like the chick of the swallow. I call her with my eyes."

She promised her mom she would come back with her uncle, and they would take her up the hill to be with her father. And she could join the stars.

"Like the chick of the goose," she sang, *"I call my mother from outside."*

But Od never made it back; she never was able to make it back to their home, or the mountain. And she worried her mother would never be with her father.

"My dear, dear child, sleep in the warm cradle, my child."

***

Over the following days and weeks, the puppy got stronger. Od sacrificed her food and own strength to nourish the dog. She named her, "Golog," puppy, fearing that any other name, might attract demons and demons would bring death.

Its other eye healed and opened, revealing another color, not the light brown but grey and hazy, without stars. "It's blind in that eye," Gan said when he saw it.

As it grew in strength it moved and would follow Od to the ladder at the bottom of the manhole. It barked when she climbed, and she shouted at it. "Quiet, Golog! They will eat you." It wouldn't stop whining, and Gan told Od she couldn't leave her.

"It echoes," he said. "They may have already heard her."

Od climbed back down into the sewer and put Golog into her coat. "Stay quiet," she said. "Please."

Od and Gan made their rounds, first, stopping to fill their bottles at the local grocer. Outside the bakery, a man saw Golog stick her head out of Od's jacket; he smiled and held up a finger, telling them to wait. He returned a moment later with a whole warm loaf of bread. He gave Od the bread and scratched Golog behind the ears. "Take care of the little beauty," he said.

The bread was warm and soft and melted in her mouth. Gan cried as he held his half and rolled bits in his hand, smelling it before eating any. After tearing a small amount for Golog, he stuffed the rest of his bread into his pocket and told Od to save it, not to eat it yet. "But it's warm," Od said, holding hers to her nose and placing small piece after small piece in her mouth.

"This is too much for us," Gan said. "We should share it with the others."

"But Golog," she said, tearing off another piece for the dog.

Gan grabbed her hand, stopping her. "The others need to eat more than your dog," he said. He took Od's half of the bread and put it in his pocket with his own half. "For the others," he repeated, as Golog whined and struggled to get out of Od's arms and at the bread.

Gan and Od searched through the dumpster across from where she had first found Golog. The puppy sniffed and dug through the trash, barking when it found something. "See," Od said, smiling. "Golog is taking care of herself." She had found a half-filled plastic bag of *aaruul*, mare's cheese. "Good girl," Od said, taking the bag and letting Golog chew on a piece.

After more searching with no luck, Gan left the dumpster. Od lifted Golog over the side and dropped her down to him, but the puppy rolled and fell out of his arms, and ran away, chasing a cat across the street.

"Golog!" Od yelled dropping to the ground. She ran across the street after the dog. A car screeched to a stop to avoid hitting her but still nicked her side and knocked her to the ground. Gan ran after and helped her to her feet, as the car honked at them. Od spotted Golog on the other side of the playground, where she had trapped the cat in a corner, and was barking at it. The cat hissed and showed its teeth. A man jogged over to Golog and picked her up, laughing as Od and Gan made it to him. "You're fierce for such a little thing," he said. "Is it yours?" he asked Od.

She nodded and reached for Golog, but the man didn't hand her back. Instead, he reached into his pocket and took out a wallet. "5,000 tugriks enough?" he asked.

"No," Od said, reaching again for Golog.

Gan pulled on her arm, "Take it," he said. "That's enough food for weeks if we're smart."

Od shook her head and started to cry. "Golog can find food for herself."

"Golog is eating *our* food," Gan said.

"10,000 then," the man said, taking the money out and showing Gan.

"Two weeks of food," Gan told Od. He held her behind him as he reached for the money. "We'll take it."

"No!" Od shouted. She kicked the back of Gan's knee and he fell, the money in his hand. Od grabbed Golog from the man, yanking her away as the puppy yelped. She ran back towards the sewer with the puppy as she heard the man shout, "thief!" Gan let out a cry as the man kicked him. The man grabbed him by the collar, lifted him in the air and took the money back.

"I'll keep you safe," Od whispered to Golog as they lay on their platform in the dim sewer.

Gan didn't return until much later and when he did, he told Od, "Golog can't sleep here anymore."

One of Gan's eye was swollen shut, and his lip was split open. A line of dried blood ran down his chin.

"Sorry," Od said. "We couldn't—"

"I told the others about Golog," Gan said. "They'll be here soon and take her away."

"No!" Od shouted. "No—why?"

"You're going to die because of the dog." Gan took his spot on the platform, laying down and closing his good eye. "They need to eat. If you had taken the money, we'd all eat and Golog would be safe."

Od cried, holding the squirming dog close to her chest. She left the sewer with Golog and ran out into the street. "I have to put you somewhere safe," she said. "Somewhere they can't find you." She shivered as the Mongolian sun set, and the streets grew silent — the cold froze the sound of Od's footsteps as she ran over the paved streets and hard dirt. She had to move quickly; her legs were numbing, her feet losing all feeling, she had to find a safe place. Across several empty streets, under a barbed-wire fence was a storage yard filled with shipping containers. She pulled on container after container door until she found an unlocked, empty one.

"Stay, stay here," she said. "Stay quiet." She set Golog in the dark container and took off her coat. "I'll be," she struggled to speak through her chattering teeth, "back in the morning." She wrapped the dog in her coat and patted her head, but the dog barked and climbed out of the coat. "No, stay," she wrapped it again. "I can't stay, stay," she said. "I'll freeze." She held Golog in the container with her foot as she closed and latched the door.

Her arms wrapped around herself, she ran back to the sewer, shaking violently. Her body floated above the concrete, her arms, legs, face, and body weightless, painless, warming. She moved through the silence like a dream, her parents running and laughing next to her. "Fast as a horse, Od!" her father said, holding her hand and pulling her forward faster. "Your skin is showing," her mother said. "It's too cold to have your skin showing."

She didn't remember getting back to the sewer or pushing up against Gan for warmth, but when she woke up, she was still shaking, and she cried as her skin thawed. Gan cursed when he woke and looked at her hands. The tips of her fingers were cracked, blackened, and bleeding. He touched them and asked if she could feel them at all. Od couldn't.

After a piece of bread for breakfast, Od and Gan left the sewer and, reluctantly, he followed Od into the storage yard, climbing under the fence when no one was in sight. "She can stay here at night," she said.

"You left her and your coat here?" Gan asked as Od opened the container, pushing up on the latch and pulling the door open.

"She needed to stay warm," Od said.

Gan lifted Od's coat off the container floor as she called for Golog. He put it on her as she moved farther into the structure. And as Od's eyes adjusted, she saw the dog in the back corner, wrapped tightly into a ball, her face buried in her tail.

"Golog," Od called, but the dog didn't move. "Golog." Od knelt next to her and placed her hands on the dog's head. It was cold. "Golog." She patted the head and shook the stiff legs. "Golog!" The frozen body moved as a solid unit as Od shook it, just like her mother.

***

"Mom!" she shouted. Her mother was stiff, and her eyes were open. And she didn't respond, no matter how loud Od yelled. "Mom!" She grabbed her arms and tried to drag her out of bed. She climbed onto the bed and pushed her until she fell, her mom hitting the ground of their *ger* with a thud. Od learned that dead things still bleed as blood came out of where her mom's head hit the floor. The stars in her mother's eyes were glazed over and gone, their light hidden by clouds.

***

Golog's frozen eye now matched her clouded blind one. Od held the frozen dog to her chest and zipped up her coat with the dog inside.

"What are you going to do with it?" Gan asked as they left the shipping yard and climbed back out under the fence. "If you can't eat it," he said. "You should give it to the others to eat."

Od didn't answer, but instead of heading back towards the sewers, she walked away.

"Where are you going?" Gan asked, He tried to grab her, to stop her, but she shook his hand off. "Where are you going?" he asked again.

"Home," she said.

***

Gan didn't follow her, and she didn't stop walking all day. She went a dozen miles across the city, through the Soviet-built districts. She passed more kids, kids in the freezing streets. Kids that were left out during the day by their parents to beg. She made it out of the city, and through Mongol-made *ger* districts, and then through trash covered slums where whole families lived together in cardboard huts, kept warm by fires. Past it all and into the country, where the wind moved over the land and carried even the silence away. As the sun set on the Mongol steppe, the cold earth ate at Od again until she felt nothing. She glided above the frozen ground, and the hill rose in front of her and she climbed. Golog's frozen body, warmed and limp, pinned tight against her chest.

The stars lit her way, millions upon millions, more than she remembered.

Her parents were with her now, encouraging her up the hill, telling her she was doing the right thing, the best thing. That she needed to place Golog on top of the hill: to honor her, to let her join the stars like her mother never could.

The further she got up the hill, the further her mother fell behind. "*Eej!*," "Mom," she called down the rocky slope.

"It's okay," her father promised. "Just keep going."

Od was growing warm, hot; she was burning. She took off her coat and left it as she continued to the top. The sun began to rise as she reached the summit, the city in the distance behind her, fires and lights fading into the morning light. Her father stood waiting, just ahead next to a pile of rocks, sticks, and blue flags. The stars faded as Od placed Golog at the base of the pile. She fell to her knees as her mom came from behind. She knelt over Od and sang, holding her and stroking her hair.

"*Like the chick of the white duck, I call my mother from far away.*"

Od laid down next to Golog as the puppy nuzzled in close and licked her face.

"*Like the chick of the swallow. I call her with my eyes.*"

And, she closed her eyes as her father sat next to her mother.

"*Like the chick of the goose,*" she sang, "*I call my mother from outside.*"

She took her mother's hand and said, "Too cold," as her mother sang the last verse of the lullaby.

"*My dear, dear child, sleep in the warm cradle, my child.*"

Mongol Boys

When I write to my friends in the States, I tell them that Mongolia is in the middle. It's the PB and J between Russia and China. But, Mongolia is actually where the world ends. It's the edge of everything. There isn't a drop, or a cliff where the ocean's water falls into nothing; it's where everything fades away.

We leave the capital, and the buildings shrink into tents and *gers*, the small white yurts that house whole families. Beyond the people, the mountains become hills, trees turn into shrubs, and the grass wilts to cracked dirt.

In the brown nothing, we find herds of horses and the occasional camel. If we didn't stop at the resort but kept going, I think the blue sky and brown ground would merge into a muddy fog.

***

Nergui throws the ball back to me. All of his throws land short, and I have to scoop them off the ground as the wind throws dust in my face. The air rumbles in my ears and I worry about not having my hat. My friend Peter once lost part of his ear due to frostbite, so I cover my ears with my hands between our throws.

Nergui, the Mongol boy, doesn't have gloves. His hands are red from the cold of the steppe and swollen from trying to catch the hard white ball.

Most of the Mongol boys I know are named Nergui. It means no name. It is supposed to confuse the demons and keep the boys from being stolen by evil spirits. The boys don't get real names until they're older and can keep themselves safe.

My parents say Jesus keeps the demons away from me, but I'm still extra careful. I don't tell strangers my name. I never step on a threshold. I don't show anyone the bottom of my feet. And I always jump into my bed quickly so nothing can grab me.

When we arrived at the resort, my dad saw Nergui kicking around a soccer ball by himself and told me to go play with him while my parents unloaded our things into the *ger* we rented for the week. I grabbed my glove and baseball and decided I'd rather play catch with him. I watched as my family went into the *ger* and made sure that none of them stepped on the threshold.

At first it was fun, and it was better than unloading, but now they're done and inside, and the cold has gotten colder. It won't be long before the sun sets, even though in northern Mongolia the sun stays low; it seems to take a long time to set. When it does, the cold is doubled by the dark.

My family will eat soon. They'll sit in the *ger*, their backs against the round, soft felt wall, nearly sweating from the heat of the stove. Our hosts will cook some mutton soup. It will smell terrible and taste bearable. They'll crack open the door because it will have gotten too hot inside.

I breathe on my gloveless hand. Ice crystals form from the water droplets on my palm. My feet are stiff and numb, but the numbness is better than the pain that will come when I warm them.

Nergui and I are completely alone. The cold doesn't seem to bother him—he smiles and laughs. Nameless and fearless, he keeps the demons away as we toss the ball back and forth.

I throw higher above his reach so he has to turn and chase after the ball. This gives me longer to cover my ears and close my eyes. I can feel the warmth of my eyelids.

Nergui shouts happily in Mongolian as he throws the ball back. It rolls to my feet. My knees are stiff. I bend and scoop up the ball with my glove. I keep my throwing hand in my coat pocket.

"I'm done," I tell him. The English hits the ground and Nergui can't scoop it up. "Duussan," I shout, but even my Mongolian is English to him. And he doesn't understand the Mongolian word for stop, so I hold up the ball and make an X with my arms.

He smiles and holds up his hands the same way, so I throw him the ball and we continue. I throw the ball high enough so Nergui can track it and catch it for once. Maybe then, we'll be done.

But he drops it. Again.

"Duussan," I shout. Maybe it's the wrong word, I'm not sure anymore.

A gust of wind sends a shock down my neck. It pushes through the numbness all the way to my frozen toes. The back of my head burns as Nergui's throw falls short. And I feel like running away.

My eyes and lips are dry. They leak and freeze at the corners. But my cheeks feel warm as I pick up the ball and imagine my family eating. The sun is sliding into the ground, and the *gers* in the distance glow with heat, their edges and shadows shimmering.

Between passes, I glance behind me. I know out there somewhere there are wolves, bears, hungry dogs, and snakes, but that's not why I look back. In the last few minutes, before the sun completely vanishes and the dark swallows everything, Mongolia turns orange.

Inside the Buddhist temples, everything is orange. On the walls there are pictures of demons torturing people, boiling them, stabbing them, removing their skin, and setting them on fire. The orange moment before dark is when all those demons come; and they stay out in the dark until the next morning. The *ger*'s threshold keeps them out, unless you step on it; then they are all let in.

Nergui is more shadow than person now. He's hidden from the demons, but I'm not. I'm white and can still be seen. I'm done, and I want to get into the *ger* and step over the threshold.

I pick up the ball, feel the stitches, and squeeze. I have to end the game. So, I throw it at Nergui as hard as I can, harder than I should.

Something snaps as it hits Nergui's face.

He doesn't make a noise, but he covers his face with his swollen hands as blood pours out his nose, down his chin, and over his hands. Finally done with the game, he runs back to the *gers*.

I'm alone as I pick up the ball. The wind moans and sighs as I run back to the *gers*, the demons chasing me, until I'm over the threshold.

***

In the morning, Nergui is nowhere to be found. My parents ask if Nergui and I had fun playing catch, I say yes and don't mention the bloody nose. When I go outside, I find red spots in the dirt and kick at them, covering them in earth.

When the rest of the mission team arrives for our annual meeting, the adults gather in one of the larger *gers*. One of the older boys, the son of my parent's colleagues, Peter, says he will keep an eye on me during their meetings. We are allowed to go out riding and my dad pays for two horses for the day. Peter assures my parents we won't go far.

My dad helps me onto the horse. "The man says this horse is a champion. Won the Naadam race years and years ago, and he did it without his rider," my dad tells me.

Peter and I ride for hours without stopping, galloping over marmot holes and chasing dust devils. My horse, the former champion, doesn't listen to my shouts, but he follows close behind Peter's horse. My butt is sore and chaffing. Despite my layers, I'm cold. I want to go back, but I know Peter will make fun of me if I tell him. He'll call me a baby. Even after losing part of his ear to the cold, he still refuses to wear a hat. I lean closer to the champion's warm, dark hair, and rest my cheek on its neck.

Far away from the resort, the world takes shape again. Large rock structures stretch out of the earth like dragon claws. A river cuts the ground, and hills rise around it, trees lining its banks. Peter leads us into a forest between the hills. This seems like a magical place. A place hidden and separated from the rest of the world.

When Genghis Khan died, he was buried with all his wealth. Treasure hunters have looked for it for hundreds of years. Everyone who knew where the treasure was hidden was killed. The Mongols even say that a river was redirected over his tomb so the treasure would never be found. I think, it must be in a hidden place like this.

It's no wonder no one has ever found it. Mongolia is so empty and big. Sometimes it feels like there is more in the sky than in the earth. At night, the stars feel connected to the world, and there isn't space and earth; space swallows the earth.

We go down to the edge of the river. It's mostly frozen, but what isn't frozen is swift and deep. We let the horses out onto the ice to drink while Peter looks for a way to cross.

"We'll have to look for a better place," he says. "It must be frozen over somewhere further down."

I pull on my horse's reins as Peter heads down the riverbank, but the champion doesn't respond. I kick his sides; however, instead of turning, he moves forward, stepping off the ice and into the rushing water.

"Zogs!" I yell, using the Mongolian word for stop. The horse pushes forward. I think about jumping off, but it's too late, and I can't swim. The champion rushes deep into the river, splashing freezing water onto my face. I close my eyes and hold tight to the horse's neck. Water surges over my legs and up to my waist. I gasp as the cold sucks the air out of me.

My teeth chatter and clank as the champion's head bobs. Suddenly I can't feel anything below my waist. I look back to see Peter in the distance. He can't hear me over the roar of the river. My white fists clasp the reigns. I'm slipping off the saddle as the champion jumps and turns back to the shore. I think how I might join Genghis Khan at the bottom. But with a lurch, he puts his front hooves on the ice, pushes up with his back legs, and climbs out of the water.

Peter must have realized I wasn't following, because he trots back as I fall out of the saddle to the ground. My frozen legs can't catch me. I crumble.

Peter ties our horses to a tree and starts a fire using the box of matches he always carries. Cigarettes are hidden in the same box. He smokes and tells me not to tell my parents about this as we dry my pants by the fire. He lends me one of his layers of pants: they're too big, so

I hold them up as I shiver next to the flames. My teeth clammer so loudly they might break.

"Stupid beast," Peter says. He flicks a rock at the champion, who rears and neighs in response, and walks around to the other side of the tree.

Peter loves baseball. "America's sport," he calls it. He's told me he's going to be a professional pitcher. He thinks soccer is a stupid sport and gets upset when I play with the Mongol boys in our neighborhood. "Hope it freezes to death," he says. He throws another rock at my horse, but it misses and hits his horse in the head.

I say we should head back, but Peter says, "We should get your blood moving. Let's go for a walk."

We follow the river, this time on foot and I begin to feel my legs again. It's painful at first and they're unsteady, but my shivers become less violent after a few minutes.

On the other side of the river is a herd of sheep. "Watch this," Peter says. He reaches down and picks up three rocks. "The small one at the end." He points to the nearest sheep. It's too far for me to throw, but Peter winds up. The first stone hits a tree and the snaps from the branches echoes over the river.

He winds up again. This time the stone hits its target. The sheep wails and runs forward, joining the rest of the herd. Peter's third rock slips out of his hand and doesn't make it to the other shore. His face gets red as he picks up more stones. He no longer winds up, but throws rock after rock, smiling at the noises coming from the sheep across the water. He stops. "Not bad, huh?" he asks.

There's another snap somewhere in the valley, but Peter didn't throw a rock. A Mongol man on a horse across the stream charges at the river. A large stick is in his hand, hanging at the horse's side. The herd's shepherd and his horse jump into the water.

Peter curses and takes off up the hill and I run after him, tripping over my numb feet as we start. We head into the trees and up the side of the valley. I glance back at the shepherd, who's already across the water and racing after us. I've lost track of Peter. He's vanished ahead of me in the trees.

I can't breathe, and I can barely move, so I slide to the ground and pin my back to a boulder. I cover my head with my arms, close my eyes, and listen as the shepherd and his horse approach. I hold my breath as he passes me without slowing down. When the sound of the horse fades up the hill, I get up and run back to the river. The thought of the shepherd's stick and the pain it would cause drives me quickly back up the stream to where we left our horses. The champion is still tied to the tree, but Peter's horse is gone. He must have beat me back and left.

The champion carries me out of the valley. I have to trust him to lead us home as the sun sets. My dad said he won the race without his rider; he can find his way. I refuse to look back, fearing that I might see the shepherd. The orange takes over as the champion and I pass the dragon's claws and the wind cries after us. I fear the demons and I wish Nergui was here to hide me from the evil spirits.

Soviet Skatepark

The first time Peter went to the black market a man slipped a hand into the front of his pants. Peter was a tall fifteen-year-old, nearly six foot. He towered over most Mongol men, but the man with his arm around him was taller. Warm breath displaced Peter's hair and warmed the back of his head. Separated from his dad in the crowd, the touch of the cold skin that cupped and fondled him left him frozen in the stream of bodies moving around him to buy stolen car mirrors, pirated DVDs, and ABBA tapes.

Since then, Peter hasn't left the house without a belt. He tightens it a notch too tight. A year later, he still gets tense and he has a lump in his throat as he pushes his way through the crowded, outdoor market. A woman at a kiosk tries to sell him fossilized dinosaur eggs. She tells him they're real and he can sell them for three times the price, and all Americans want to buy them. He believes her for a moment, before refusing and moving on. He has 20,000 tugrik with him, and he's not here to buy anything but a knife. His father refuses to let him have one, asking, "Why would you need a knife?"

"For protection," Peter answered.

"Did Jesus carry a knife?" his father responded.

Peter made an argument about the wild dogs on the streets, but his father dismissed him. "You've been fine this long without a knife."

Peter keeps the money in a small bag tied around his neck. He knows the slight tugs on his pants are hands slipping into his pocket, and now, he cares less, knowing they'll find nothing.

"Khutga," Peter repeats to himself. This morning before leaving the house, he found the English to Mongolian dictionary on his parents' shelf and memorized the word for knife. "Khutga."

He finds a kiosk set up with various bows and arrows, hand-carved staffs, and a stack of Bruce Willis head-shots. The owner points at Bruce Willis and tells him 500 tugrik.

"Khutga," Peter says. The owner arches his brow and slowly repeats "Khut-ga".

Peter stabs the air with a closed and titled fist. "Khutga."

The owner smiles and reveals from under the table a sheathed hunting knife. He takes it out and shows its curved tip and serrated base. "50,000 tugrik," he tells Peter.

"15,000," Peter says.

"30,000." The owner touches the point and Peter nods and pretends to understand what the man is saying.

"20,000," Peter says. He doesn't swallow or even breathe as he locks eyes with the owner. He doesn't want him to know that he can't go any higher.

The man nods and stretches out his hand, waiting for payment. He's smiling.

"If they're happy," his dad once said, you've lost the barter.

But Peter doesn't care. He takes the small sack of coins and paper tugrik tied around his neck out of his shirt and exchanges the money for the knife. He sheathes it and ties it next to the sack. He keeps his hand on the knife as he leaves the market.

The Soviets built Ulaanbaatar, without knowing much about the Mongols. They poured concrete, built walls, and fences, trapping the once nomadic people. Unmoving and unchanging apartment buildings in square districts, enclosing parks. The only thing that changed was the type of park. Some have basketball courts. Others gravel soccer fields. Between the black market and Peter's family's apartment, they built a skatepark. It's three acres of concrete, sunk eight feet below the base of the surrounding buildings, completely fenced with a single entrance that's locked and goes unused. The kids in this district climb the fence and help each other up and down the eight-foot drop. The ocean of concrete is scattered with plyboard islands, ramps and half pipes, some as high as two stories.

The Soviet's forgot that the Mongols don't have skates, skateboards, or bikes. The Mongol kids play soccer between the structures and chase each other over the wooden waves.

Peter climbs the fence and takes a seat on the edge of the skatepark. Below him a dozen kids, five to ten years younger than him, play soccer. He hasn't ever played with them. His dad and him tried starting a baseball league when they first moved here from the states. There were several kids, but his dad got busy and Peter had to teach them how to play on his own. The kids failed to learn. They didn't have gloves, and his nice wooden bat was stolen twice, both times reappearing for sale in the black market. The first time his dad reluctantly bought it back and told him to keep a better eye on it. Peter gave up trying to teach the Mongols. They were more interested in soccer, anyway.

One kid misses the goal wide right: the ball bounces and rolls to a stop below Peter. He drops down and picks it up. The kids hold up their hands, waving for him to return it. Instead, he takes his new knife and pushes it through the ball. It pops and shrinks; he tosses it towards them like a frisbee. The children yell, and one shows him a middle finger, but none of them follow Peter as he makes his way across the park to his family's apartment building. He pulls himself out of the concrete hole and climbs over the fence. Outside his building, he finds a plastic bag. He places his knife in it. Then, on his knees, digging in the dirt with his hands. He puts the bag in the hole and covers it. He moves the dirt around the spot and memorizes the location. Once he's sure he won't forget which tuft of grass it's next to, he heads back into his apartment building.

His family lives on the seventh floor, but he never takes the elevator. Sometime long ago it became a bathroom, and, for Peter, the stench is unbearable. He takes two stairs at a time. At the metal door, Peter listens with his ear pressed next to the doorknob. The neighbors have a goat tied outside their door. It pushes up against his legs and hits its hooves on the ground; the clanks keep Peter from hearing anything inside the apartment.

He opens the door and slips inside.

"Where have you been?" his father asks. His shoes are on and he's slipping on a coat, a large coat, too big and too warm for the Mongolian spring, which had just seen the ground thaw.

Peter sets his light jacket on a hook and says, "I was in the skatepark."

"You're supposed to tell us whenever you leave." Peter's father grabs his arm and looks at his hand. "Why are your hands dirty?"

Peter looks down at his father, who's barely halfway to six foot. Peter's mother is six foot, and Peter hates being seen in public with the two of them, as the Mongols gawk. "I fell," Peter says.

His father's face grows red, starting at his cheeks, moving to his forehead, and finally, down his neck. "Your mother was worried." He lets go of Peter's arms.

"That doesn't sound like mom." Peter's mother didn't worry about anything but his younger sister, Maggie. At fourteen, she's still not allowed outside by herself.

"Kitchen," his father says, "nose in the corner until I say." His fists are clenched, and so red, they'd burn if touched.

Peter locks eyes with his father and bites hard, clenching his jaw. As his father shakes and opens his mouth to shout, Peter moves to the kitchen.

His mother is sitting at the table reading a book entitled, "*Shepherding a Child's Heart*". She doesn't look up as he enters, or as he takes his place in the corner, his nose touching the adjacent walls.

Peter thinks of all the time he's spent in the corner. He could have taken piano lessons with that time, read hundreds of books, learned to draw or juggle. Instead, he's memorized the patterns of the plaster, drawn constellations in the deformities and traveled on journeys through mountains made of dimples. He's learned how to endure the ache in his knees that comes from standing for hours, by shifting his weight from leg to leg.

After an hour, or hours, Peter can't tell, Maggie comes into the kitchen.

"Dad says you can leave the corner and come with me to the store. We need bread," she says.

Peter rubs his eyes. His mother's no longer in the kitchen. Maggie's dressed for the outdoors, her shoes already on, a shopping bag in her hands, and a black lace head covering (a triangle piece of cloth that Peter's father insists that Maggie and his mother wear whenever they leave the house) holding her hair back.

Peter points to the bread on the counter. "We got some yesterday," he says.

She puts a finger to her lips and slips the bread into her shopping bag. "Do you want to stay in the corner all day? Come on."

Peter follows her out of the apartment, grabbing his jacket and closing the door quietly behind him.

"What did you do this time?" Maggie asks. She gives the neighbor's goat the leftover bread. "He's cute, huh? I've named him Billy."

"Couldn't think of anything more original?" he asks.

Maggie punches his arm. "It's a good name."

Peter makes Maggie wait as he finds the spot that he left his knife. He locates the tuft of grass and uncovers the plastic bag.

"So that's what you were really doing this morning," she says as he takes the knife out of the bag and shows her. "You really do love that corner."

"It's to keep us safe," Peter says.

Maggie laughs. "From everyone but dad."

To get to the store, they walk around the skatepark. They put their hands to the sides of their faces as the wind picks up and carries dust down the concrete corridors. Spring wind brings dust up from the desert and piles it in the city.

They pass a group of men smoking on the stairs outside the store. Peter understands why his parents won't let Maggie out alone. The men's heads turn, and their gaze follows as she walks up the stairs and through the door. His hand in his pocket, Peter squeezes the hilt of the knife, but none of the men come into the store after them. The smell of fresh bread, sweet, warm, and soft, releases Peter's grip on the knife.

Maggie buys two loaves; she holds them to her nose and smiles. "They're so warm," she says. "Touch them." She takes Peter's arm and puts his hand on the bread. She thanks the baker; her Mongolian is better than anyone in the family, despite her limited contact with Mongols.

"Why the second loaf?" Peter asks, as they pass the men on the stairs, his hand back on the knife but still warm from the bread.

"For us, of course." She hands him a ripped piece of the bread, smiles, and takes a bite straight from the loaf. "It's best warm."

Peter and Maggie take the long way home, making a full circle around the skatepark. On the far side of the skatepark is the sixth district where the Russian embassy is located. Peter scales the wall that separates the districts, jumping his fingertips on the ledge. He pulls himself up and then reaches down and pulls Maggie onto the wall. From the top of the wall, the two can see into the Russian embassy's courtyard. Young Russian kids swing on swings. The older boys shoot hoops on a basketball court, and the older girls walk around a green garden, an oasis in a desert of grey and brown.

Peter and Maggie eat their bread. They've named all the kids. Each one has a story and they have their favorites. Maggie likes one of the boys playing basketball; the one with short blonde hair. He's taller than the others, but he acts kind, and plays as much with the younger kids as with the older kids. She's named him Zach. "He seems sad today, doesn't he? Like some big decision is weighing on him."

"And, what decision is that?" Peter asks, chewing on the cooling bread, salty and smoky. He takes out his matchbox from his jacket where cigarettes are often hidden. Lighting one he tosses the match asise and offers Maggie one. It's no suprise she refuses. She always refuses.

"They're having a dance, and two girls like him, but he has to ask just one," she says.

"They have dances in the Russian embassy?" Peter asks.

"Shut up," she says. "Of course they do." She leans on her hand and tilts her head. "He doesn't want to choose either though."

Peter laughs and coughs. "Let me guess, he only likes American girls?"

Maggie shakes her head. "Don't be stupid. He's too mature for both of them. He wants someone he can really connect with."

"I guess it's hard to dance with someone you don't really connect with?" Peter smiles and jumps down from the wall. "Come on. Let's get you home, before mom worries."

Peter and Maggie cut through the skatepark to get home.

"Bitch!" a kid yells as they make their way. It's a small kid; Peter thinks it might be the one who gave him the middle finger earlier. He turns to confront him, but Maggie grabs his arm and says, "Ignore him. He doesn't know what it means."

"He knows it's an insult," Peter says.

"He's just a kid." Maggie pushes him forward and they keep walking.

The boy keeps yelling 'bitch' after them, louder as they ignore him.

"Tegit?" Maggie calls back. "It means, 'so,'" she tells Peter.

But the boy doesn't stop. He picks up stones and starts skipping them on the concrete at Maggie.

"Knock it off," Peter says. He takes the knife out of his pocket and the kid drops the rocks. "That's what I thought," he says. The kid backs away.

"You shouldn't scare him like that," Maggie says as Peter gives her a hand up and out of the skatepark.

Peter holds up his hand for Maggie to grab. "He shouldn't—"

"Bitch!" the kid yells again. A stone flies over Peter's head and hits the side of Maggie's face. She gasps as blood trickles down the side of her cheek. The cut is dark on her pale skin.

Peter feels faint. His hands are shaking as he takes out his knife.

"Peter, I'm fine," Maggie says, but he doesn't listen. He runs after the boy.

The kid's fast but Peter's legs are longer, and without help the kid can't get out of the skatepark. Trapped, the boy tries to hide behind the ramps. Peter chases him beneath a series of half pipes, into a dark, enclosed section of one plyboard structure. Light comes through the ceiling in rays from rotten holes. Blankets are piled in corners, trash in others, and the familiar stench of urine is thick. It was someone's home, or still is, but only the boy is here now, coming into focus as Peter's eyes adjust to the light.

The boy shouts as Peter steps towards him. He throws the only rock in his hand, but Peter ducks and it clangs off the plyboard. The boy charges. Peter swipes down with the knife. The boy screams, his right ear flapping, hanging loosely from the side of his head. He falls to the ground, crying and bleeding.

Peter drops the knife and runs out of structure and doesn't stop. He walks as he gets close to Maggie. She holds her hand to her cheek.

"I heard a scream," she says. "What did you do Peter?" Her eyes are wild, her gaze darting from Peter to the direction of another of the boy's screams.

He doesn't answer. He pulls himself out of the skate-park, and grabs her wrist, pulling her back toward the apartment.

"I fell," Maggie said, as they climb the stairs. "That's what we'll tell them. Okay? I fell."

Billy the goat isn't outside the neighbor's door anymore, only his leash, still tied to the doorknob.

***

"I tripped on the steps up the store," Maggie tells their father.

His face as red as Maggie's cheek, he says, "And it took you this long to get back?"

"It's not that bad—"

"I'm looking at it," he says. "I can tell how bad it is. Go get it cleaned up!" He grabs Peter's arm as Maggie leaves. "And what did you do as your sister bled out? Took your sweet time to get her home?"

"We came back right away. She—"

"You think I'm that stupid," he says. "The corner. You can leave it when you're ready to tell me the truth." He twists Peter's arm as he starts to walk away. "And you smell like smoke."

The plaster constellations aren't the usual. He sees his father's angry face. Maggie's cheek. The men on the stairs watching. The boy flipping him off. The boy's ear. The knife. His knife. He left his knife. He had to get it back, now. Someone would take it, like his bat. And he might never see it again.

There's a knock on the door. "John," Peter's mom calls, "can you get the door. I'm helping Maggie."

Someone might have seen him with the knife, and found the boy, followed him here. Peter listens to his dad answer the door, trying to understand the Mongolian, but his pulse pounding in his ear muffles it. He can't understand anything but the tone, which sounds friendly. Peter sighs as the front door is closed and his dad comes into the kitchen.

"The neighbors gave us some goat meat," his dad yells to his mom down the hall. He places the plastic wrapped hunks of meat in the fridge and leaves. "Nice of them, huh?"

His steps fade down the hall, Peter knows this is his chance, and that he may end up looking at this corner for the next week, but he can't lose his knife. He slips out of the kitchen and to the front door, opening and closing it quickly and quietly.

Billy the goat is still gone, and Peter thinks about how upset Maggie will be when she finds bits of him in their fridge.

Peter runs down the stairs, out the apartment, over the fence and down into the skatepark. It's empty now. Unusual for this time of day, he figures the wind and dust must be keeping the kids inside. He has a sickening thought as he heads for the spot that he left his knife that the boy might still be there, bleeding, or worse, dead.

He slows to a walk and looks to make sure he's not being watched. "It was just his ear," Peter tells himself. "It was just his ear." He enters the dark plyboard structure and the noise of the wind is gone, and he can hear his heavy breathing. His eyes take time to adjust; he sees drying blood but the boy is gone. He takes a deep breath in relief, feeling light. He searches for his knife. He tears through the blankets and the garbage, and crawls around on his knees, but it's gone.

There are voices outside. He gets off the ground and moves to the entrance. Three Mongol men, in their late teens to early twenties, move from ramp to ramp, half-pipe to half-pipe, yelling back and forth. The largest of the three holds Peter's knife.

Peter returns to the dark and listens, as the voices get closer. He thinks about making a run for it, for the edge of the park. It would take time to climb out, and if they saw him, they'd catch him for sure.

The blankets. Peter pushes the trash and blankets into one corner of the space. He covers himself with the pile, lying down and pressing himself against the urine stained playboard, his nose touching the wood.

Footsteps. Someone enters the structure. They move around the space. Peter holds his breath and focuses on keeping completely still. The man shouts, calling for the others.

Peter's instinct is to run, but he resists and remains frozen, thinking he couldn't have found him; he's hidden.

The other two join the first in the room. They shuffle around and yell at each other. They've seen the blood. Peter closes his eyes and prays for an escape, remembering stories of missionaries saved from persecution. Suddenly, the three-stop arguing. They remain silent as a pair of feet scrap across the concrete.

Peter is grabbed by the shoulders and pulled out of the blankets. He tries to get up and run, but a second man grabs his waist and throws him to the ground. Peter coughs and tries to roll onto his stomach, but his arm is grabbed and pinned. He pushes the man with his free arm and screams. The first man grabs his other wrist, twists it back and onto the ground.

Peter cries. "Please, stop!"

The third man stands above him, holding his knife. Peter kicks at him, but the other men put their weight on him, and he can't move anything but his head. "No! Stop! No!" Peter yells again and again as the third man kneels over him and holds his head in place. His voice cracks and he wets himself. The man puts the knife to Peter's right ear and slices it in half.

The men leave him on the ground. They leave the knife. They take his ear.

His hands covering and pressing on the left side of his head, he sobs and shakes. The fresh blood covers the old.

The Healer

"He hasn't been eating. Nothing stays down," my translator explained after listening to the man lying on the couch. House visits were a new approach. We found it was easier for the more seriously ill.

Qudan was pale and he groaned as he rolled over and looked up at me. On the small table next to the couch was an empty bottle of vodka and another half-filled. "He's not drinking while he's like this, is he?" The translator repeated my question to Qudan. He grunted his answer.

"He can't stop, he says." My translator pointed to the bottles on the table and said, "He's never been able to stop."

"Well, that solves that mystery." I bent down next to him. "He has liver disease. I think it's shutting down. He's going to die."

My translator started to repeat what I said. "Stop. Don't tell him that, Monkh." I pulled him into the hall. "We can't do anything for him. We shouldn't have come here. He's too sick to heal."

"He has offered a lot of money," Monkh said, peeking back into the room. "He has no family. No one will know it did not work."

"It's risky," I said. "It only takes one failure to lose all faith."

"He is offering a lot. 500,000 tugrik."

"Alright," I said. "But when he dies? What do we say?"

"We say it was punishment," Monkh said. "God giving punishment for his drinking."

I moved back into the room and knelt by Qudan. I set my Bible on the table next to the vodka and placed my hands on his face, resting my thumbs on his eyes. "Lord, your humble servant, Qudan, begs for your healing. His sins have left him in this state." Monkh repeated the phrasing. Qudan's eyes watered, his warm tears rolling over my thumbs. "We know your power, Lord. You promise to heal your people, if only we ask, if only we trust." Monkh hovered above us. I looked back at him as he smiled.

Monkh never believed any of it, even when I still did. It was Monkh's idea to monetize the healings. I was reluctant, but once we started, I found there was something in the investment that helped the sick. Somehow believing they were part of the healing helped.

I had seen God do miracles with my hands. And there was a time I believed it was God's power making the lame walk, curing cancer, and making the deaf hear. But it wasn't. It was me. It was my belief in my ability to heal that made it work, and more so, my ability to convince them that they were well and *could* be healed.

We collected our money and I took the half empty bottle of vodka with me as we left Qudan's apartment. I stuffed my half of the money into a hidden sleeve in my Bible.

Before we left, Qudan told us he felt brand new; he even stood up, moved off his couch, said all the pain was gone, and ate a full meal for the first time in weeks.

***

I took a sip of the vodka and threw it into the dumpster outside the apartment building. Monkh led me down the cold concrete street to another apartment, where we had another scheduled healing. We climbed three sets of steep stairs towards a piercing scream. "It is a young girl. Her parents believe demons are inside of her," Monkh explained to me. "She has violent moods. They tie her down so she will not cut herself."

We knocked on the door and an elderly man answered. He fell to his knees and grabbed my legs, mumbling Mongolian praises.

"Get up," I told him. "It's alright. Show me your daughter."

The man grabbed my hand and getting up, pulled me inside the house. Monkh reminded me to remove my shoes as we followed him to a closed door. His wife stood next to it, listening to the screams and crying.

"Help her," the mother said. "Help her," she begged. Monkh translated as I opened the door and instructed for the parents to wait outside.

We entered the musty, dimly lit room. The young girl was sitting on a chair, its back against the radiator, her arms tied to her sides. I closed the door behind us.

The girl thrashed about, her head flinging dangerously close to the concrete wall and the scalding hot radiator. Blood trickled down her cheek from a cut above her left eyebrow. She shouted at me, her eyes wide and scared.

"She is calling you a–"

"No need to translate," I told Monkh. "Stay back a bit. And talk calmly to her. Try to mimic my tone." I took a deep breath. "What's her name?"

"Nekhii."

"Nekhii," I repeated. I moved closer, slowly. I took a handkerchief from my pocket and offered to clean her cut. "Tell her, it's okay. Tell her, I won't hurt her."

Monkh repeated my words as I kept my gaze locked with hers. Heat buzzed off her sweaty body and made me sweat, too. She either had a fever or had been left by the radiator too long. Her clothes were damp, and the smell of mold and festering flesh made me gag, but I did my best to hide it.

***

I took my Bible from my pocket and set it on her lap. She stopped shouting and only stared as I wiped the blood off her cheek. I moved to the restraints on her hands and began to untie the ropes.

"Bad idea," Monkh said.

"It's okay," I said. The girl remained silent as I took her hands and flipped them over to look at her arms. Old and new scars ran from her wrists to elbows. I put my hands softly over the scars, my cool hands resting on her warm, marked forearms, and I closed my eyes. "Almighty King and Lord, your daughter Nekhii is hurt. Heal her, take the pain, cleanse her from the evil within, show her your love and acceptance."

I opened my eyes and looked at Nekhii. "You're well," I said. As Monkh repeated my words, she smiled and, shaking, gave me a hug.

I told Monkh to bring in her parents. They wept as they hugged a somber Nekhii. They thanked me for returning their daughter. We took their money, and thanked them for their offering, promising to use the money to help more like their daughter.

I stuffed my half of the money in my Bible. "Call the police," I told Monkh, as we went down the now silent flight of stairs. "I think someone is hurting that girl."

***

I came to Mongolia to help the people. I thought I could heal them. I heard stories of their need, of their illness and poverty. The poorest and sickest lived in the sewers and in the trash heaps; they were kept warm by others' excrement and garbage. I couldn't help them spiritually, not when they physically couldn't cope with life. They needed the very basics before I could hope to move on to any sort of talk of God, or love, or Christ. When I was in seminary, I had a blueberry muffin and a latte when I listened to lectures on Christ's love.

So instead, I prayed over them for God to provide; however, they died anyway. In his name, I commanded the sick to get up and walk and they fell. But, here in Mongolia, it didn't take much success to garner attention. My teacher and mentor at seminary told me healings are easier in places where the need is greatest because the people truly believe. Truly hope. It's why I came to Mongolia; I had heard their need.

***

"How did it happen?" I asked Monkh on the way to another appointment.

"He doesn't say," Monkh said. "So, I asked others. They tell me he was caught with another woman, and his wife took a knee to him. More than one knee to him."

I had become quite familiar with the Ulaanbaatar hospitals. We entered Songdo Hospital and Monkh told the receptionist who we were looking for. "It sent him to the hospital? How serious could it be?"

"He is not expected to ever be able to have children," Monkh said.

"Ah, that kind of knee taking. What kind of healing is he expecting?" I asked. "I can't uncrush his parts."

"He wants a miracle."

The man in the hospital bed pulled on my hand and spoke quickly. "He's asking if your God can give him a child," Monkh said.

"His wife did this to him," I said. "You think children are still a possibility?"

Monkh frowned at me. "You want me to ask him?"

"No," I said. "Let's just get this over with." I took both of the man's hands and knelt next to him. "Father, this man—"

"Terbish," Monkh said.

"Father, this man, Terbish" — the man squeezed my hands at the sound of his name — "he has sinned, and you have punished. Lord, I ask you not just to heal him, or only take the pain from him." Monkh repeated my lines. "I ask Lord that you restore his ability to procreate."

***

"I hate this," I told Monkh on the elevator on the way back to the first floor. "We're not healing any more testicles. Okay?"

Monkh pulled the money out of his pocket and shrugged. "Money is money," he said and gave me my half.

At first, I took only enough donations to feed, cloth, and shelter myself. But Monkh had found an increasing amount of work. I sent most of my cut back to the States, to my ex-wife and son.

I'd feel guilty if the healings didn't provide anything. But they provided hope, a placebo, and at least momentary relief. Monkh said that if the healings didn't hold, it just meant more work and double pay. And if it still didn't hold, or they were unsatisfied, we offered refunds and more to keep them quiet. But the longer we continued with the healings, and the larger the amount of cash in my Bible, the greater the guilt grew.

"I can't keep doing this," I told Mokh as we sat in the back of a taxi, heading out of the capital towards two brothers who severely injured themselves in a game of Kakbar. Monkh explained that the game involved two players on two horses and a tug-of-war match over a fox or goat pelt. I asked him how this could possibly be our first Kokbar-related healing. "This is our last one," I said.

"Why?" Monkh asked. "Do you need to return home?"

"No, this is wrong. I can't keep taking these people's money," I said. "Not when there are kids in the sewer, and look" — I pointed out the window at one of the hills, where smoke billowed — "people live in that dump."

Monkh smiled. "I have a solution. I know how to give some of the money we make to those people."

"Some of the money? We should only keep what keeps us fed and housed," I said.

"Yes," Monkh agreed. "You give me the money, and it will get to the people in the trash."

Just outside the capital, the boys' mother led us into their family *ger*, out of the cold and into the salty warmth. She took us to her sons. They laid head-to-foot on a thin, twin-sized bed.

The two brothers couldn't have been older than five and six. The younger had lost the Kakbar match to the older and sustained a head injury. Under the bandages was the top curve of a hoofprint just above his eyebrow. The older was had his own injuries – a broken nose, cracked ribs, and a broken and crooked arm that obviously needed to be reset.

"These boys need actual medical attention," I told Monkh as I looked over the boys. "Can they afford to take them to a hospital if they pay us?"

Monkh whispered to the mother and she whispered back. "They can afford it just fine," Monkh assured me. "She wants you to try to heal them."

"If they could afford it, why didn't they fix this boys arm?" I asked.

Monkh shook his head.

"I'm not a doctor," I said.

"You are a healer. Heal," Monkh put his hand on my shoulder and said, "Heal, for their mother."

I looked behind him. The boys' mother covered her mouth, her eyes welling up as she watched me. I took my Bible from my coat pocket and placed it on the bed. "Dear Lord, these young boys need your healing. They–"

The older boy opened his eyes and squinted at me. He moved his hand onto my Bible and whispered something. I waved Monkh closer. "What's he saying?"

Monkh spoke to the boy and he whispered again. "He says to save your power, and only heal his brother."

"Tell him God's power is limitless," I said. "He is more than able to heal them both."

Monkh explained but the boy pushed my Bible away from him and towards his brother.

"Heal him," the boy said through Monkh. "Heal him."

I moved to his brother and gently put a hand on the youngest's head. With my other hand on the Bible, I prayed for the children. And for the first time in months, I prayed with intent. The boy reminded me of my own son, though he was a lot older now. I used to pray with him, kneeling by his bed before he went to sleep.

I stood up to leave and the older boy rolled over and my Bible fell to the floor. Monkh picked it up. The boy reached his hand out to me and asked if his brother would be alright. If I had saved him. I squeezed his hand and said we'd have to wait and see.

As we left, Monkh gave me my Bible back. I told him not to let the mother pay. "They need it," I said. "In fact," I reached into the Bible for my money, but it was gone.

"What is it?" Monkh asked.

"My money," I said, checking my pockets and the ground around me.

"The boy," Monkh said, walking to the *ger*. He yelled at the mother, who let us back inside. Monkh and the mother shouted back and forth, as they moved to the bed, removed the blankets, and searched around the *ger*. The older boy cried and the younger stayed asleep. The mother dragged the older boy out of his bed and threw him at my feet, his twisted arm limply hanging from his side. She kicked him and yelled.

"Stop," I said. Monkh was still searching around and under the bed. "Monkh!" I yelled. "Tell her to stop!"

Monkh slowly moved from the bed and stopped the mother, but not before she was able to kick the boy again. The *ger* door had been left open and the heat at been sucked out. The boy shivered on the floor, his broken nose bleeding again. He repeated the same thing over and over.

"He says he didn't take it," Monkh translated.

"It's fine," I said. "I must have lost it elsewhere. And if they did take it, they can have it. They need it."

I felt sick and threw up before we got back into the taxi and again while on the road. Monkh paid the driver extra for the mess.

***

"Do you have other money to give to people living in the trash?" Monkh asked when we arrived at my apartment.

I nodded and once in my apartment, I gave him all the money I had, only keeping enough for rent and food for the week. He took it and said he'd get it into the right hands right away. But I still couldn't sleep. I stared at the ceiling and heard the boy's cries.

Our next trip was to a dying elderly woman. Monkh explained the situation; the lady's family wanted her to live to see her granddaughter's wedding this summer, but doctors told them she wouldn't make it to spring.

"We're striking out," I told Monkh as we walked through a gate and up an icy path to a secluded apartment complex. "Not one of these recent healings will hold."

"They have lots of money," Monkh said, ignoring me and watching the guards.

"Liver failure, mental illness, impotence, head trauma, and old age aren't healings you can fake," I said. "When they realize that our help did nothing, they'll be after us. We won't be able to do this anymore. No one will pay."

Monkh greeted the guards and held the door open for me. "These people are old Mongolia rich. Soviet Union rich," Monkh explained. "The people who live in these apartments must have had important government jobs before the fall." He touched the white walls and stopped to look at the paintings, landscape pieces of areas across Mongolia — mountains, lakes, deserts, and rolling green hills — each one with a perfectly clear blue sky.

We knocked on one of the apartment doors and a young Mongolian woman opened the door. The dress was western. I could imagine my ex-wife having worn it.

"Welcome. I am Tuya," she said. "I know little English." She smiled at me and then turned and spoke to Monkh.

"She says, thank you for coming. She wanted to tell you that her grandmother is resistant to this. That she is Buddhist." As we walked down more white hallways decorated with images of American cityscapes - San Francisco, New York, Chicago, Seattle - Tuya explained that she had traveled to the states several times. That she loved the country and she and her husband hoped to live there one day. Tuya convinced her grandmother to see us because she had attended churches in America and seen amazing healings done with simple words.

She led us into a living space where her grandmother sat in a recliner, a felt blanket across her lap. Her eyes peered at us through swollen eyelids. Her face was sketched with a permanent frown.

"*Sain baina uu*, hello," I greeted her. She didn't answer. "I hear you're sick," I said.

Monkh translated and the elderly woman replied with a laugh, her large wrinkly frown curling up.

"What's funny?" I asked.

The woman stopped laughing and talked to me.

Monkh listened. "She says, she is just old, and that you can't help her. That we bring evil into her house."

"Tell her, if she only believes, God can heal her," I said.

The old woman spoke and Tuya scolded her.

"She says that if she already believed she was healed, she wouldn't need us. Tuya is telling her that she promised to try this." Monkh told me.

I took my empty Bible from my coat and placed it on her lap. I held out my hand for her to take. And after some encouragement from Tuya, she placed her hand on mine. "Lord, all knowing, all powerful, all loving, Lord." I gently squeezed her hand. "Lord, this woman comes before you with a simple request, to replenish her strength, to allow her to live to see her granddaughter's wedding." I waited, listening to the Mongolian repetition of my words. "She may not believe in your power, but change her, make her believe by showing her a miracle."

I took my Bible back and placed it in my coat pocket. But her grip on my hand tightened when I tried to let go. She said something slowly and clearly, her eyes moving from mine back to Monkh, I glanced back at him for the translation.

"An old saying," he said. "Do not make yourself blind cleaning your eye."

"Don't blind yourself cleaning your eye? What does it mean?" I asked.

"Not sure. It's only a saying," he said. He turned to Tuya and after a brief conversation, she handed him a large wad of money.

Tuya's grandmother let go of my hand but not before repeating the saying again, as Monkh counted the bills. Tuya thanked us and we left. Monkh asked if I wanted my half or if I'd rather this payment go straight to "the people in the trash".

"Keep it," I said. "But Monkh, can I see how the money is being used?"

He stopped walking. "Right now?" he asked.

I nodded. "Yes," I said. "I would love to."

"Not today," he said. "I will show you tomorrow. I will pick you up."

Before I could question him further, Monkh began explaining how happy they had been to receive the money - how they had bought warm clothes and food and praised my name. He told me they would be excited to meet me.

We returned to our homes, and the next morn-ing I waited for Monkh, but he never came. Eventu-ally, I got a taxi and went to his place. I knocked, but no one answered, so I went to his neighbors and tried to ask them if they had seen him. I had to repeat his name over and over for them to understand what I was looking for, but they shook their heads. After asking the neighbors on the floors above and below, someone took me to the apartment manager. He went with me up to Monkh's apartment and, having seen me there before, let me in.

"Monkh?" I called. The apartment had been cleared out. The drawers were empty and the cupboards bare. And Monkh was gone.

I sat on the frozen stairs outside his apartment and flipped absently through my empty Bible. I was looking for something, anything, some sort of sign, when a man across the street slipped on the ice and fell. He let out a cry of pain and held his knee. I ran over and knelt next to him.

"I can help," I said. "I can heal you."

His eyes darted around, and he called past me to others along the road as he curled up and rolled in pain, cupping his hands over his knee.

"I can help," I repeated, hoping the repetition would help him understand. I showed him my Bible and held it above him. I was crying, happy for the sign, as I put my hand on his shoulder and prayed, shouting, "Lord! Heal this man. Show me your power, heal him and let him walk!" I stood up and pulled on the man, lifting him to his feet. He stumbled forward. "You can walk, you can walk!" But with another cry of pain, the man fell again.

I froze as he cried. He shouted at me and I dropped the Bible, and fell to my knees next to him, calling others on the street for help.

A History of Mongolia

"*Oui, oui,*" Sophie said. "It is *magnifique!*" She pulled Maggie closer to the ice sculpture of the Eiffel tower. "*Bonjour!*" she yelled at the Mongolian artist standing next to his creation.

"*Sain uu,*" Maggie told her. "*Sain uu* is hello."

"But I'm learning French, not *magnolian.*" Sophie smiled at the man and said, "It's really good, sir."

"Mongolian," Maggie said.

"Mon-go-lee-an," Sophie repeated. She turned away from this sculpture to another and shrieked at the dragon. Its mouth hung open, revealing rows of translucent teeth.

Sophie's brother Thomas was already standing next to it. Fog left Thomas's nostrils in jet streams, raising into the air and dissipating. Maggie thought he looked more like a dragon than the sculpture. Mongolia's winter cold made everyone moving around the square look like steam engines, puffs floating above their heads.

"*Magnifique!*" Sophie shouted again. This Mongolian artist didn't speak French either, but the smile on Sophie's face left him grinning as she walked around the muscular limbs in awe. "How do they do it?" Sophie asked Maggie. "It's magic? Isn't it?"

"They collect the ice from lakes, and carve, chiseling away to find these beautiful works," Maggie explained.

"I bet it's not that hard," Thomas said. He shivered. His arms crossed as he moved away from the dragon. "Can we leave yet?"

"No!" Sophie pulled on Maggie's arm. "I want to see them all."

"We'll see some more," Maggie said, "And then we can—"

"Look at that one!" Sophie let go of Maggie's hand and ran to the center of the square, passing ice archers, world wonders, and cartoons. She stared up at the statue of a man rearing back on his horse.

"That's not ice, dipwad," Thomas yelled after her. Maggie and Thomas followed her to the statue, and he read the plaque at the base. "It's a metal statue of suck-butter." He chuckled to himself. "Suck-butter."

"*Sukhbaatar*," Maggie corrected. "Ignore him, Sophie. This is Damdin Sukhbaatar. This square is named after him. He fought the Chinese-."

"Like Mulan?" Sophie asked.

"Mulan was Chinese, stupid," Thomas said.

Maggie stepped between them and said, "Sukhbaatar is a hero of the Mongolian people, a brave leader who fought against the Chinese in the 1920's to help Mongolia become an independent country." Maggie had spent time researching Mongolian history, but she wasn't able to find much information in English. Most of what she did learn was from Ulaanbaatar's National History Museum, where Maggie was taking Sophie and Thomas.

Thomas and Sophie's mom was a close friend of Maggie's mom. When her marriage hit a rough patch and she needed to get away from her husband, she decided to go as far as she could. Maggie's mom, the Christian missionary in Mongolia, came to mind, and a few weeks later Maggie was babysitting their family's guests.

***

She hoped seeing Mongolian culture, art, and history would help them understand what made this country so great. Stopping to see the ice sculptures in the city center was the first part of their education.

"Can we get out of the cold?" Thomas asked. "I can't feel my fucking toes."

"Language!" Sophie cried. "Mom's going to be so mad."

"I said, freaking."

"No, you didn't. You said the bad one." She stuck out her tongue at him.

"Careful, it'll freeze that way."

She retracted her tongue, frowned, and pulled on Maggie's arm. "You'll tell mom he said the bad one, right?"

"Let's get out of the cold," Maggie said. She led them out of the square and across the street to the capital commerce building. "Before my brother Peter went back to the states, we would come over here to get the best corndogs," Maggie said. "They're incredible."

They passed through glass doors and warmed as they moved into the foyer. It smelled like a slaughterhouse, wet wool and flesh. Fresh meat was being cut and moved around on tables while sheep's legs, rib cages, and hunks of fat were traded for fistfuls of paper tugriks.

Sophie's eyes grew wide and she turned pale as she watched meat being thrown from vendor to vendor. She stared at a pile of sheep heads.

It was only Thomas and Sophie's second week in Mongolia, they had yet to see this type of market. Maggie had gotten so used to being in these markets, she didn't remember what the first time was like. Americans didn't see their meat like this.

"I'm going to be sick," Thomas said, pinching his nose.

Maggie pushed through the people. She dragged Sophie behind her and trusted Thomas to follow. A butcher called to Maggie in Russian, holding up a bag of mutton. "No, thank you," she told him in Mongolian. He laughed in surprise and went back to trimming fat off a carcass.

"Whatever you're getting us," Thomas yelled. "It better be cooked."

"Here they are." Maggie stopped next to a rotisserie machine stuffed with rotating corn dogs. "They're so good."

"They look weird," Thomas said. "Sickly." The corn dogs were covered in square bumps.

"They're bits of potato. Like a corn dog wrapped in french fries." Maggie pulled out her purse tied around her neck and said, "Shoot. I spent all I brought on the taxi," she answered. "Thomas, do you have any money? I can pay you back when we get home."

He sighed and took his pouch from around his neck. He reached in and took out a roll of 20,000 tugrik bills.

Maggie covered the bills, hiding it from the corn dog merchant. "Where'd you get all of that?" she asked. "How much do you have?"

"I don't know. Not much. Mom said each twenty is like seven bucks," Thomas said, pulling the money away from her and flipping through the bills.

Thomas and Sophie's mom had no problem throwing money around. "It might not be mine soon anyway," she had whispered to Maggie after handing Thomas several thousand tugriks to buy an overpriced baseball cap and a new jacket at Ulaanbaatar's new Korean mall.

Maggie bit her lip and looked around, but no one seemed to be paying any attention. "It's not safe to carry around so much money."

Thomas held up the bag by its strings. "I'm keeping it around my neck, no one can pickpocket—"

"Just take out one bill and keep the rest tucked away." Maggie grabbed Sophie and pulled her close, saying,

"Don't make a big deal about it, or you'll get us in trouble."

Sophie shook her head and said, "I'm not sure I'm so hungry." She continued watching the chopping around the foyer.

"No one cares. You worry too much," Thomas said. "We'll take three," he said to the vendor. He handed him the 20,000.

"*Gurav*," Maggie repeated, holding up three fingers.

The vendor passed them each a corn dog.

"Actually, I want two," he said.

Maggie pointed to the machine and said, "*neg.*" The man grabbed another and gave Thomas his change. Maggie thanked the man and led them out of the commerce building. She made them wait around the corner to make sure no one was following.

"This is awful," he said. "The potatoes aren't cooked, and the meat tastes like baloney." He had already finished one and was chewing on the second.

"It's delicious," Sophie said nibbling on it. "But the sheeps lost their heads." She looked on the verge of tears. "This isn't one of the sheep, is it?"

"No," Maggie said. "It's not sheep."

"You said this was the best corn dog you've ever had?" Thomas asked. "I guess you've never had an *American* corn dog," Thomas said. He licked the first corn dog stick clean and tossed it to the ground.

"This way," Maggie said. She led them on a shortcut through an alley toward the National History Museum but was stopped when a manhole cover just ahead moved.

"What the hell!" Thomas hid behind Maggie as the manhole cover slid to the side and a child climbed out. The muddy, tattered shorts were all that kept the boy from being completely exposed to the cold. He yelled down the hole and another boy climbed out. Together they pushed the cover back over the hole and took off down the alley.

"Ack, that's disgusting," Thomas said. "They live in the sewer? They smell terrible."

Maggie had gotten used to seeing homeless kids on the streets, beggars missing legs and arms, and she'd been outside the city to the dumps where whole families lived in makeshift cardboard homes and kept warm by burning trash.

"Are there more down there?" Sophie asked.

"God, I hope not. Creepy enough with just the two of them." Thomas stayed as far to one side of the alley as he could as he moved past the metal cover. "Let's get out of here before more climb out."

Maggie moved to the manhole. "Help me lift the cover," she told Thomas.

"That's disgusting. I'm not touching that."

"Hold this for me." She handed Sophie her half-eaten corn dog. Maggie got down on her knees and placed her fingers into the small holes. She felt the heat rising from below and pulled up on the cover. It was heavy, but Maggie was able to inch it out of the hole and slide it to the side. The smell of sewage mixed with the cold air and Maggie gagged. She put a finger under her nose and yelled down the dark hole, "*Sain baina uu.*" Maggie's own voice echoed back from under the alley.

"Well, that's freaky," Thomas said. "I'm not waiting for more creeps to crawl up, I'm going to go see this museum you've been raving about."

"Give me the corn dog," Maggie said. Sophie stepped closer to her, leaning forward and risking a peek down. Thomas did the same and hovered above the dark. His money bag slipped out of his shirt and hung above the hole. Maggie thought about all the money in that bag, and all it would buy the kids, all the clothes, and all the food: if she had that money, she would give it to them, and at least today they wouldn't be hungry.

Maggie took her corn dog from Sophie and set it on the ground next to the manhole and pulled the cover back in place. She stood and brushed herself off.

Sophie placed her slightly nibbled corn dog next to Maggie's.

"I'm not leaving mine," Thomas said. "Some animal will just eat it anyway." He took another bite and they left the alley.

***

They entered into the warmth of the museum through thick wooden doors, and Maggie wondered why the sewer kids didn't spend their time here. It was open to the public and it even had restrooms. If they didn't have the *tugriks* to pay to get all the way into the museum, they could still stay in the foyer. No one seemed to be watching the doors. The sewer kids could even hide in here at night. One of Maggie's favorite books was about two children who ran away from their home and lived in the Metropolitan Art Museum. But she noticed a security guard walking down the hall and wonder how he would treat the kids.

Thomas took out his bag of money again, this time removing it from his neck to get the smaller bills and coins left over from the corndog transaction. He gave the money to Maggie and she paid for three tickets.

"Don't forget. You owe me for the corndogs too," he said. Maggie noticed he didn't bother putting the money back around his neck; instead, he slipped the bag into his pocket. She opened her mouth to tell him it would be safer back around his neck, but she decided not to. If he lost the money — if it was stolen — it would be his own fault.

"What's first?" Sophie asked, skipping forward into the poorly lit room, with hulking stone obelisks. She stood next to the largest, staring up at it, under its shadow. "You brought us to see rocks?"

"Well, Mongolia may screw up corn dogs, but they got stupid rocks down," Thomas said. "Look at this one, Sophie." Thomas pointed to the second-largest rock. "It's exactly the same as the other, but smaller." He laughed and Sophie frowned.

"They're ancient rocks," Maggie explained. "A long, long time ago, ancient Mongolian's carved out this stone and put images—"

"I don't see any images," Sophie said.

"They've faded now, but if you can imagine—"

"Is there anything else?" Sophie asked, following Thomas through a hall and into the next room.

"Sophie, wait," Maggie said. "Listen." She put one finger to her lips and another to her ear. Soft music was playing from speakers in the corners of the room. "It's *Boris Godunov*," Maggie said, smiling.

Maggie and her parents would attend the Russian opera whenever they were performing in Ulaanbaatar. They were the highlights of Maggie's years in Mongolia. For a few days, the city was cultured. *Boris Godunov* was her favorite. They had seen it last winter, and she had liked it so much that Maggie's parents had bought her the opera on tape.

"This is my favorite opera," Maggie said. "Do you like opera? We can check to see what's playing before you go home to the states."

"You listen to this for fun?" Thomas asked before Sophie could answer.

"Have you ever listened to Russian opera?" Maggie asked Sophie. "It's like a play but they sing the whole time. This one is in Russian."

"Are there any French operas? That would be *magnifique!*"

Thomas had continued down the hall. "Hey, Sophie!" he called. "Look at this! It looks like Rover!"

Sophie ran over to the stuffed, shaggy brown dog with glass eyes. "It's beautiful," she whispered. She ran her hand through the dog's fur. "It feels just like him too.

How they make it look so real?" She looked at her hand, some fur still stuck to it.

"It is real," Thomas said. "It's dead."

Sophie wiped her hand on her pants and tears formed. She ran away down the hall.

Maggie shot Thomas a look as she followed Sophie.

The Russian music filled the entire museum. Maggie appreciated the museum's taste but wondered why more traditional Mongolian music wasn't being played; it was the *Mongolian* National History Museum after all.

She recognized the scene the music was dictating. It was the part where a Polish noblewoman seduces Grigori to gain power so that Russia's new leader would be Catholic. The opera shows immoral actions being used to help the church — evil being used for good. She often thought about the terrible things that happened here in Mongolia, the terrible things the Mongols did and let be done — like the kids in the sewer. Yet, somehow, all these things could be working for good. It was even beautiful in some way. She smiled, thinking that some of that good might have been her leaving the corn dog for the kids.

Maggie didn't rush to find Sophie, who had darted around the hall corner. She took her time in the hall to look at each work of art. Mongolian art was unlike any she had ever seen in the States. It breathed and moved, and the green landscapes vibrated with life. She believed Mongolian artists must be connected to something bigger, something more powerful than themselves. Maybe it was something evil — demons or witchcraft. The type of evil the Mongols believed moved around the countryside. But with it, they could create something beautiful.

Maggie was here to appreciate their work when others hadn't or wouldn't. It was like Maggie's family. They had come here to help the Mongolians. They weren't like Thomas or others who came to take advantage and leave. And they weren't like the Mongolians who seemed fine to ignore their own people.

She caught up to Sophie. A Mongolian man was also in the room. He leaned over a display labeled 'Weapons of the Horde.' Arrowheads, bows, and knives filled the glass case.

Sophie sat on the floor under a painting of Chinggis Khan. She rested her chin on her hands and pushed her cheeks up to her eyes. Maggie sat on the floor next to her.

"Magnolia sucks," she said. "I want to go home."

"Back to our apartment?" Maggie asked.

"No," Sophie said, looking up at her — her eyes big, brown, and watering. "Home, home."

"Tight," Thomas as he entered the room. "This is more like it." He looked at the Chinggis Khan painting. "He doesn't look so tough." He turned and looked at the rest of the room and said, "Check out this dude." He jogged to the stone casket on the other side of the room. "Compare that fat guy and this little dude. Do you think all that fat just melts away when you die? What do you think, kid?" Thomas helped Sophie to her feet. They moved next to him and looked inside the casket at a small skeleton.

Maggie got up and came behind them to look into the casket. The protruding ribs reminded her of the that climbed out of the sewer. The skeleton's skull was caved in. The plaque above the casket explained how the cause of death had been a blow to his head.

The Mongolian man's attention was now on Thomas. Maggie could see him watching from the other side of the room. He looked familiar. She wondered if he had been in the marketplace and if he had followed them.

"Maybe that Chinggis guy could have given this guy a few pounds." Thomas laughed. He leaned back, stuck out his gut, blew up his cheeks, and waddled forward. He skipped like he was on a horse, his sack of money nearly falling out of his pocket as he passed Maggie. The bag's string hung from his pocket. Maggie grabbed the string and the bag slipped out of his pocket. Neither Thomas nor Sophie noticed.

"Let's go conquer China!" Thomas yelled.

Sophie laughed, wiped away her tears, and followed him into the next room.

Maggie thought about keeping the bag of money. She could take it to the kids in the sewer. She could find them and tell them to buy food and clothes. They'd thank her and maybe even love her.

The Mongolian man in the room was going on to the next display. Maggie thought about dropping it on the ground. He'd find it and take the money. That's probably why he followed them anyway, to take the money. She couldn't take it, but she knew the Mongol man would. It would teach Thomas a lesson. He hadn't even given the sewer kids his corn dog and now it would cost him.

Maggie kept her chin high and her gaze above the ground and dropped the money bag as she went into the other room.

But she was stopped as the Mongolian man called out, "*Khüleekh!*" He pointed to the bag on the ground. He jogged over, picked it up, and handed it to Maggie.

Thomas and Sophie watched, Thomas feeling around in his empty pockets.

The man smiled at Maggie as she took it, and then handed the bag to Thomas.

"Uh, thanks," he said.

Maggie didn't look back, she continued further, but Thomas stopped her.

"Hold up," he said. He ran back after the man, pulling several bills out of the bag. He got the man's attention and offered him the money, but the man laughed and refused. Thomas smiled as he came back. "What a nice guy," he said.

Maggie stayed back from the other two as they marveled at the Mongolian fashion exhibit, and she wondered if evil could still be used for good.

"*Magnifique!*" Sophie yelled at the Mongolian dresses and hairstyles.

Diesel

Diesel freezes. We start fires under the trucks in the early morning and thaw the fuel tanks. We pack our trucks with skinned sheep, piling them into the back. By the time we return, the women will have turned the wool into felt. And we'll have new blankets, gloves, and hats. They're already boiling the wool down, filling our homes with thick, earthy steam.

It's a five-day trip to the capital, so we pack extra diesel into the cabs and under our feet. We'll ride with our knees to our chins, and take turns driving so we can stretch our legs.

We have three trucks in total, packed with our season's load of mutton. We'll return with medicine, toys for our kids, diesel, and coal to last the winter.

The children and women line up before we leave to see us off. They nod at us, the twelve men, four to a truck, as we get into our vehicles, and they watch our caravan until we pass over hills and vanish from sight.

Our trucks are alone with the sky and the soft wind. We follow dirt paths that our ancestors have traveled annually for thousands of years, northward, toward the city, over plains and through the desert. The wind howls and whispers to us, letting us know that we approach lands where demons and ghosts wait.

Vultures circle our trucks as snow begins to fall. We argue about whether to turn back home, whether we have enough diesel to make it back and try again, whether we should wait here for the night. We stopped the trucks and swear at the vultures, and we ask if they are an omen warning us or evil spirits cursing us.

We don't have enough diesel to go back. And if we don't keep moving, the tanks will freeze and we'll have to warm them up again. So we continue forward and so do the vultures, and as we descend into a basin, the sun sets and the vultures fade, but the snow in front of us grows. Instead of a sky of stars above for us to navigate by, there is a sky of black. The snow makes it look like the stars have come to earth, and now they are in front and all around us.

We move forward in a line of three. Nugia leads our pack, driving the truck in front. He doesn't slow down or stop all night, so neither do the other two trucks.

When the sun rises, it only blinds us, filtering through the snow creating an otherworldly white, a place of spirits. The earth below frozen and the wind shouting. We can see no further than the truck in front of us, and even that fades in and out of view. We honk to make Nugia stop, hitting the horn over and over to be heard over the wind. He stops and with his hand on the side of the truck, so he won't lose it, he walks back to us.

We tell him he is going too fast, and we can't keep his truck in sight. He tells us he's lost the path. The snow has covered it. Yul, in the middle truck, suggests we wait out the storm. But we tell him it could last for weeks and if we stop the diesel will freeze. And in this wind, we could never start a fire, and in this cold, we would freeze without the heat of the cabin in half a day. Turgen in the last truck says the demons will be on us if we don't keep moving.

We move our trucks forward at a crawl, only an arm's length from hood to bumper. At these speeds, the engines don't make the heat they did, and the cold seeps through the windows, and ice clings to them. We sip vodka to stay warm. And Ulagan drinks more than he should and tells us he sees his ancestors in the white mist. He tells us they are frozen to their horses, with beards of ice and black eyes. We shake him awake when he falls asleep. And when he has to relieve himself of all the vodka, we stop the trucks to let him out. But he wanders too far.

We shout his name but only the wind screeches in reply. "Ulagan!" We move around the trucks, hands locked together, always keeping someone touching the truck's frozen metal. The cold burns our eyes and we shiver and shake, our teeth clacking. We return to the cabs. We don't move the trucks, but we keep them running to be sure they won't freeze. Soon we will freeze if we don't move.

We take turns returning to the cold and shouting. But with each passing hour, the cold grows stronger, and the white mist out of our lights' reach turns grey and then black. We know but we don't say that Ulagan must be frozen. We move the trucks and leave the spot.

Turgen says he can hear Ulagan's children crying outside the trucks, begging us to stay, to find their father.

Nugia keeps the truck in front at a steady pace. He insists that we keep moving. We only sip the vodka, no one risking judgment for warmth by taking more. And we do this for another day and use a full tank of diesel. We wrap our faces with felt scarves as we fill the tank again with the diesel in the cabs, draining all our reserves. Ice forms and fuses the inside of the scarves to our faces, and we have to peel the felt off as it melts.

"This is our punishment for leaving Ulagan," Turgen tells us. "This storm was sent by the ancestors he saw." Turgen moves to the second and third truck, making the blind leap between vehicles with his arms and hands reaching.

"We didn't leave him," Nugia says. "He left us. There was nothing more we could do."

"This is our hell," Turgen says. "This is our punishment."

"Get back to your truck." Nugia turns back to the car.

"I see him." Turgen points out into the snow. "Ulagan, calling from the white."

"The cold's going to your head," Nugia said. "Vodka will do you good."

He forces Turgen to take a drink and makes him return to his truck. We watch him stumble his way past the first truck, but he trips as he moves past the second, falling face first into the snow and lying motionless. We jump out of our cabs and carry him to his truck, and we wrap him tightly as he shakes. He barely breathes as we cut the ice from his face.

Nugia rethinks his strategy, as going forward has gotten us nowhere. And we whisper that we're going in circles, but none of us know. It's the same white blindness in every direction. He instructs the eleven of us to stop moving and to fire up the engines every twenty minutes, and let it run for five minutes to keep the diesel from freezing.

We breathe steam into the cab, filling it with our breath, and we smile and tell stories as we pass what is left of the vodka. We boast of our mightiest feats. Sukh tells of his bear hunt. His trek across the south and the Gobi, tracking the rare *Mazaalai*, killing it with an arrow to the heart, and bringing the pelt to his wife-to-be's father. He showed he was a mighty warrior and worthy of a mighty woman.

Yul confesses how he come to join our group. How he disrespected his family, stole his father's horses and his brother's wife. How he ran thousands of miles from the northern mountains and the frozen lakes to our home in the eastern plains.

Our youngest, the newest man of our group, coughs after taking his first swig of vodka. And even he laughs as we share memories of our first drinks.

Our story sharing moves to confessions, and we see dead ones in the mist, frozen black hands on the windows, and we hear voices shouting in the wind, calling our names, and reminding us of our wrongs, our failures, and our fears.

"The demons know our names," we say.

We try to convince ourselves that it's the cold moving into our heads, but that only scares us in a new way, almost more than the spirits.

We drink too much, through another night, just to keep from shaking. We run the trucks' engines, on and off, and our hearts freeze when the engine clunks and won't turn over, but when it does, our hearts beat with the engine. Steam rises from the vents and out of our mouths.

When the sunlight returns and the vodka is gone, Nugia tells us it's time to move forward. The blizzard shows no sign of slowing, and with our diesel running low, our only chance is to make it out of the storm. The wind has kept the snow from piling, instead, the ground moves in white waves. The desert turned ocean.

We trust Nugia. He is our leader. He is the strongest and bravest. The best hunter and father of the most children. But we think about other times he has led us astray, times he has moved our herds to barren, brown lands, lands he promised would be green. And the lands ahead look barren.

We start our trucks and follow Nugia, but Turgen honks his horn, signaling for us to wait. His tank has frozen. He waited too long between his warm-ups and the diesel froze.

Negui tells him we'll leave the truck, and take the other two, and try to find it once the storm has passed.

"The mutton," Turgen says. "We can't leave it. We need it."

"It won't fit on the other trucks," Nugia says. "We'll come back for it."

"We'll never find it." Turgen refuses to leave the truck, telling us that without the mutton and the money from selling it, our families won't survive the winter.

Nugia tells us our families won't survive if we die and if we don't move we will freeze. We spend longer than we should arguing and trying to start a fire under Turgen's truck. The wind is too strong and blows out our matches. Our toes freeze, our knees stiffen, our skin cracks, the tips of our noses and ears grow black, and we rub our eyes to keep them open.

Nugia tells us he's taking his truck forward, and others can decide for themselves whether to stay or go. Turgen stays with his truck, promising the storm will soon pass, and he will see us in the capitol. Yul stays with him, but not because he thinks the storm will pass. He stays with the back truck because he believes the storm is for him, his punishment, and that the only way to save his family is to let the storm take him.

At Nugia's bidding, we unload the mutton from our truck and onto the ground next to Turgen's truck. "The diesel will last longer with less weight," he tells us.

"You're killing all of our families," Turgen tells him. "Now, we will all freeze."

"Without us, they will," Nugia says. He hugs him and returns to his truck. We leave the piles of mutton, and Turgen and Yul, and continue forward in the storm.

Through the white, we think about our people. Our families back in their *gers,* waiting for our return. When we don't return, they will know why. They know Mongols freeze all the time out here. They get stuck —trucks break down, the horses trip and injure themselves, spirits confuse them. And, they get lost — run out of fuel, they starve, and the cold takes them. They stay grounded. They are the reason for the storms and wind. Their fear, their pain, their shouts, their screams, their spirits fill the land with wind and keep the snow trapped.

Now, we will join them.

With nothing to navigate, we fear we're lost. We could be heading home or going toward the capital. Or worse, we could be heading towards nothing at all. And if that is true, even if we make it out of the storm we could run out of diesel and freeze under a clear sky.

The cab warms as Nugia speeds up, determined to find our way out. And we scream in pain. Because it is never the freezing that hurts, it's always the reheating. The pain comes as the blood circulates and brings feeling back to the places that were nearly dead.

Sukh fell in the snow while unloading the mutton. His bare hands disappearing and returning to sight with ice clinging and penetrating his flesh. His hands swelled, red and twice as large, but now as they reheat, and water swells in his eyes, the hands that killed a bear turn black with death.

We sip the little water we have left and nibble on the last of the dried strips of meat as another day passes by. Not long into our fourth night, our back truck runs out of diesel. So, we have to leave it and pack into Nugia's truck.

However, the nine of us can't fit into the cab that was only ever meant for three. Four of us have to stay, knowing there is no chance, no heat. Sukh volunteers, telling us that without his hands, he might as well be dead. Our youngest volunteers, trying to prove himself brave and worthy of our group, but we refuse to let him. The other three men are chosen by rolling bones. They accept their fate and tell the five us to take care of their families, to keep them warm and safe. To tell them they died bravely. We don't prolong our goodbyes, the cold cutting them short. We leave them behind.

The five of us left sit on each other's laps and push our backs against the windshield to fit into the cab. We still feel the cold through the window and our clothes. We stay silent and focus on breathing slowly and calmly. The air is stiff and suffocating, and it gives us thoughts of jumping out of the truck, because there's more air out there, in the dark, white nothing.

The tank is nearly empty. Nugia tells us it will only last until morning if we continue forward, but it will last another day if we sit and wait. Again, we have to decide whether we stay and try to outlast the storm or push forward.

We take a vote, and three to two, Nugia the deciding vote, we continue on. We mutter quiet prayers through the night, whispering to the wind, letting it take our words to our families. We tell our sons to be strong and brave, to work hard and take care of their mothers and sisters. We tell them to be relentless and sharp, to treat the earth well, trust their instincts — that those feelings are us — their fathers and our fathers, guiding them.

We tell our daughters to find men that can hunt and provide. Men that can keep them warm in the winters and smiling in the summers. Men that can raise their own children to be wise and strong.

We apologize to our wives, for leaving them alone, for not providing them with food and warmth. For not being wise. For letting demons distract, tear us apart, blind us, and lead us to death.

Morning comes and with it sight, not clear, not perfect, but we can see into the distance. As the sun's light filters through the storm, we can see the ground and white hills around us. We make it to the edge of these hills as the truck runs out of diesel. We know our only hope is to try and find help. And the only way we can do that is outside the storm. So, we leave the truck and move in a line up the hill. As our stiff limbs and shivering bodies reach the top, the snow clears in front of us. The wind dies.

Barbarians

"Most brains are deprived of the chemicals they need," my cousin explained as we waited to enter the viewing room. "When we dream the whole brain comes alive. We call it hallucinating, but it's actually the brain connecting. Lots of different things can do it. You just need the right chemicals. Hallucinogens. Adrenaline. The feeling of being in love? — Lydia, that's chemicals. Endorphins. The body needs these chemicals. It's why when a woman gets pregnant, she gets flooded with new chemicals."

"That right?" I asked. I looked down at my phone. *You miss Lydia,* the message read. Bayar's first text arrived the moment my plane landed. It took me twenty hours from the news of my grandmother's death to pack and get flight tickets, and thirty-six hours of buses and planes to travel across Asia and the Pacific to get to this funeral. His text affected my stomach more than any turbulence. I turned my phone off quickly to make sure no one had seen.

"Stay with me," my cousin said. "We came from apes, right? Apes ate mushrooms. They weren't discerning. They just ate whatever. Some ate the bad ones and they died. But *some* ate the right ones. Now get this, their brains, they grew." Jeremy smiled as he continued, "How do you think we evolved so quickly? Our brains connected. And our cranium size doubled and here we are, humans. Humans are the result of apes eating hallucinogens."

My cousin, two years my elder, was wearing sandals and white socks at our grandmother's funeral. His paint-splattered jeans were a sharp contrast to the rest of the extended family's black attire and my black dress. His glasses made his eyes look twice as large, giving his face an insect quality, further reinforced by his yellow, crooked smile.

"You know the bible story," he said. "Of course, *you* do. The one where Adam and Eve ate the forbidden fruit. But what if the fruit didn't grow on a tree? What if it was sprouting from the base? Something you eat that gives you knowledge? What do you think it was? Follow me, are you with me? It was a mushroom."

I put my back to the wall and typed, '*Thanks*' in Mongolian. '*It should read, "I miss you, Lydia." And I miss you too.*' I sent the message and wondered how long it would take to make it to the other side of the earth, nearly the exact opposite side of the world. I thought about how, if I stayed here, Bayar and I would never see the sun at the same time. And If I didn't look at my phone, I could just vanish. He would just vanish. I looked up and said, "Fascinating. Really."

"I haven't done any dairy in over three years," he said as we stepped closer to the viewing room. "But I had a glass of milk about a month ago, and I broke out. There was acne all over my face. Zits, just everywhere. On my shoulders and all down my back. And bad, smelly farts. What you eat really can affect you. Now, follow me on this one, because it's a hundred percent true." He ran his fingerless hand through his salt and pepper hair, pulling it back, and said, "Since I started my micro-dosing, my hair isn't receding. It's growing back. And all my grey hair is turning back to black."

It was the first time I had seen Jeremy since going to Mongolia, almost five years. It was the first time I'd seen him with any grey hair. The first time his right hand was without fingers. I had heard about his accident in an email from my mother. Jeremy was a carpenter and smoked marijuana daily. The combination had made him a little too comfortable around table saws. He showed up at the emergency room but forgot to bring his fingers.

My phone buzzed and I glanced at the kissy-face emoji Bayar had sent.

"Still with me?" Jeremy asked. "There was a recent X Games contestant that won while on shrooms. And NASA was all on shrooms when they sent a man to the moon. And the secret to Silicon Valley? They've been micro-dosing for over a decade." My mom left the viewing room. She didn't look my way. She'd barely looked at me or said a word since I'd arrived. My dad trailed behind her and gave me an awkward thumbs up as he said, "She looks good. Well, as good as can be expected." He nodded at Jeremy and left the door cracked for me.

"You're up," Jeremy said. "I'll catch you on the other side." He wiggled his fingered hand in front of my face and added, "Don't get spooked."

"Alright then," I said. I entered, shut the door behind me, and took a deep breath, resting in the silence before remembering the open casket across the room.

Grandma was missing a finger too, the stub hidden under a towel. In the weeks before her death, she had bitten her ring finger, her rotten brain mistaking her flesh for food. The infection was treated with amputation. But it didn't stop the illness from spreading, and pneumonia took her two weeks before Christmas.

"It only took a death to get you home for the holidays," my dad joked when he picked me up at the airport.

I stood over my grandmother. The dust floated above her in a ray of sunlight that warmed her wax-covered cheeks. I ran my fingers down the side of her face. The last time I saw her she told me, "Stay away from the men." Her racism wasn't new, but always shocking. "Do they serve *human* food here?" she asked loudly while looking over the Chinese restaurant's menu. I should have taken her out for burgers. She turned and whispered to me, "They'll all look for a chance to take advantage of a rich, white girl. And anyone white is rich to those people."

I hated her because I hated that the same thought was in my head. And every time I interacted with a

Mongolian man I instinctively withdrew. And the Mongol women didn't want to be friends; they were kind but wouldn't spend time with me. They had chores and children, and didn't trust me, having no chores and no children. And the other missionaries all had families, I was an outcast even with them. That's why I got so close to Bayar. I needed someone. And, I wanted to prove to myself that I could get over whatever prejudice I had. I would just have to become friends with him. He was so sweet and eager to learn. It was an innocent friendship. My grandmother would never understand. Not before and, obviously, not now.

"You're giving up any chance of getting married. You're not so young anymore," she said. My mother said the same thing. I tried to tell them thirty-three was hardly an old maid. But I overheard my father tell his young doctor, "This is your chance. You better make a move quick."

I told them I wasn't giving up the chance at anything. I was choosing to sacrifice marriage, love, and sex, for God and Christ. Like Paul, I was willing to give up those things for the furthering of the kingdom. I was *called* to be a missionary. I knew it from the time I was young, when I dreamed of finding unreached people in the Amazon or Papua New Guinea and bringing them the joy I found in Christ. I would be like Paul and the other heroes of the Christian faith. But Paul and those heroes never had Bayar in their bed, sneaking in late and leaving early.

***

Her wax skin was cold and hard. Her lips stiff. She wore the slightest smile, an unnatural sort of smile because she never smiled. But she did always find joy in being right, and she was right. I should have stayed away from the men.

***

"You're teaching English?" another cousin, Alison, Jeremy's older sister asked. "To kids?"

I swallowed a bite of enchilada and answered, "All ages." After the viewing and the funeral, our family had decided to lunch at a nearby Mexican restaurant. "*Do they have human food?*" I imagined my grandmother saying as I looked over the menu. Her presence was missed at the table with her children, where they talked about their favorite childhood "mom" stories. Our table of grown grandchildren seemed content to ignore her absence. My mom watched me from the end of the table as my aunt whispered in her ear.

My uncle offered to buy everyone a margarita. I was the only one of twelve aunts, uncles, and cousins to turn him down. "Right," he said. "Missionaries don't drink."

"You know, Jesus drank wine," Jeremy said, as he licked the shaved ice off the top of his margarita.

"Isn't it lonely by yourself?" Alison asked. "I can't imagine coming home to an empty home every day." She put her hand on her husband's arm as he scooped up his cheese covered beans. "Nick was gone for a few days last week. I had to have friends over every night. It was eerie, the house all empty. Totally silent."

"And by friends," Nick said. "She means bottles of wine."

"Hey," Alison hit his arm. "Two bottles over four days. That's hardly getting sloshed." She rolled her eyes and looked back at me and asked, "Do you have many friends? Any Americans? Or just the natives? Any men?" The deeper she went into her drink, the less her eyes stayed focused on mine.

"There are a few Americans. Other missionaries," I explained. "But none are my age. And, I do have a few Mongolian friends. Men," I said. Then the lie struggled out, "and women."

"I heard," Jeremy interjected, "that Asians don't use deodorant. They use garlic to clear their pores. I think they're on the right trail. All those chemicals, seep through the skin and affect the brain. You have to be careful what you're putting into your body. It can change you. Better to be natural. Chemicals cause illness. You should read all the research on cancer causes. It's truly mind-blowing." He leaned in closer to the three of us. "Get this, I've had this terrible tooth pain. The dentist said it was nerve pain, and I needed some two-thousand-dollar surgery. I said, no way. So, I've been taking *Lion's Mane* instead. And, get this, the pain is totally gone. I got totally rid of it in a week."

The chemicals I took *did* change me. The birth control gave me debilitating headaches and depression. Though, I can't be sure that the depression was the pills' fault. Either way, I had to stop taking them. I should have just bought condoms, but having the fail-safe felt like giving into temptation without even trying to resist. Without them, I could convince myself it wasn't premeditated, that it was impulsive and somehow more forgivable.

Alison ignored her brother and asked me, "How is the language study? Are you learning Chinese?"

"Mongolian, actually," I said. "And it's slow. It's not an easy language to learn. But, as I teach English, it helps me learn Mongolian. It seems like a fair trade."

***

"*Ugui.* No," Bayar said as I corrected his paper. He had a habit of trying to convince me his bad English was good. "Bread," he said, tapping on the red circle.

"Red," I said. "Bread is food." I mimed eating a sandwich.

"Red is food," he insisted. "Bread." he kept his finger on the circle.

He wasn't the fastest learner, and two years of study had left him with little more than a toddler's understanding of directions, numbers, and colors. I remember leaning close to him, looking over his papers, his breath on my neck. His eyes following my hand as it moved across the handout. He was always interested in me and keen to understand everything I said. My ninth graders in Washington were never as keen.

"Follow me on this one," Jeremy said. "I went to Spain a few months ago but I've never taken Spanish. It was at that same time I started with the *Lion's Mane*, and I was almost instantly able to understand everything. I picked up all kinds of words and phrases, overnight. I'm not trying to convince you or anything, but you should really think about it, Lydia."

"I'll look into it," I said.

"How'd you meet your friends?" Alison asked. "I watched a documentary about this Russian family that had been completely isolated for a generation. And interacting with them had to be done with finger drawings in the dirt, just so they could figure out their words for simple things like *tree* and *house*."

Lying in bed on a Sunday morning, Bayar's back facing me, I would draw with my fingers on his dark skin. Tracing trees and homes and saying the Mongolian words and then the English. Pressing my finger harder into his back and laughing if he started to fall back asleep.

"I had a translator at first," I said. "So, it was a lot simpler than all of that."

"Sounds like that alien movie with that redhead," Nick said as he shoveled rice into his mouth. He brushed his face with his napkin, ridding himself of the grains lodged in his ginger beard.

"Amy Adams," Alison said.

"Yeah, *her*." Nick winked at Jeremy. "Anyway, she decodes the alien language and figures out that they're going to murder us all. Who knows, maybe you'll save the Chinese from the barbarians."

"Just like Mulan!" Jeremy shouts. The three of them laugh and I smile.

Bayar and I watched Mulan together. And I did my best to translate. He cursed as an avalanche took out the Hun army. He jumped up from the couch, crossed his arms, and spit on the floor as Mulan's rocket hit Shan-yu, the Hun leader. I had to coax him back to me, my hands on his shoulders, kissing his neck, lost with him, forgetting why I was in Mongolia.

Later that night, however, I would wake up and ask, *what if I get pregnant?* Every night, I lost sleep. I imagined coming home to my parents with a Mongolian man's baby in me. Then late periods and sick mornings turned my thoughts to knives, needles, and pills. Who could I tell? Bayar smiled in the morning. I didn't want to confuse him; it wasn't about him.

He didn't have guilt. Even when he was leaving before the sun rose, closing the door, the handle still fully turned as it shut, letting it go softly and slipping down the apartment stairs. As long as no one knew, he said. We were fine.

I had to end it. I knew I had to end it as soon as it began. But if he gets angry? If he tells someone? *Western women are loose. White women are prostitutes.* I would confirm everything they already thought.

And if there was a baby? Bayar would say it's okay. He'd stay with me. But his family would condemn his actions as much as mine. And I reminded myself of this on those nights, laying in the dark, listening to his breathing and feeling his warmth. At least we were in this together.

I fasted for penance and I prayed. I begged for repentance and for a way out. But I never made him leave.

I passed on dessert as the others helped themselves to churros with a chocolate dipping sauce.

"Follow me on this one," Jeremy said. "Chocolate is an aphrodisiac, right?"

Alison groaned as she took a bite, holding her hand under her chin to keep the sauce from dripping. She rolled her eyes back and said, "Heaven. It's just heaven."

"Heaven," I had said to Bayar after one of our nights together. "*Tenger,*" he had told me. The irony of me coming to the Mongolians to teach them of heaven and one of them teaching me wasn't lost on me. The guilt stuck.

Jeremy put his hands together and pointed at me. "Chocolate was originally only drunk. It was mixed in an alcoholic sauce by the Aztecs. They believed chocolate had magical qualities. It was a gift to them from the gods. A gift to commemorate life's big events. Birth. Death. Etc." He took a bite and continued. "And, get this, they would even give their chocolate drink to the people they were about to sacrifice. To cheer them up."

"I'd die for more of this dipping sauce," Alison said, waving at our waiter.

"They would even mix the blood of sacrificed victims in with the drinks." Jeremy smiled. "Fascinating, isn't it? Which reminds me of something I read about the Mongolians! That they do blood pacts. They think it makes them brothers or something? They drink yak's milk, and each member in the pact puts their blood in the milk. Then they all drink it, and they're like, blood brothers."

"Something like that," I said. "Maybe."

"That is barbaric," Alison said. "Sounds like a good way to catch an STD to me. You've never done that, right?" She dipped a churro in Nick's dipping sauce, and he moved his bowl farther away from her. "We wouldn't want you catching anything." She looked me up and down slowly.

"I've never been put in that situation," I said. "I'm not sure that is a common practice."

"Well, if you ever do contract any sort of illness. From blood or whatever," Alison said. "I know a wonderful doctor here in Seattle. She normally works with pregnant women, but I'll give you her information before we leave."

I had seen a doctor in Mongolia not long ago. My pregnancy paranoia had led to late-night reading on pregnancy websites and the appearance of symptoms. I found one piece of information particularly disturbing — 'Vaginal bleeding can take place during early pregnancy and be mistaken for menstruation.' I was fatigued. I was nauseous. I had pain in my pelvis. My stomach was bloated. I constantly needed to use the restroom. However, I wasn't pregnant. I couldn't be. I took pregnancy test after pregnancy test, only to be haunted by the idea of false negatives (something common for expired imported Russian brand tests).

I set up the appointment to clear my head. I needed to know for sure. For better or worse, it was better to know. And if I was? I would have to marry Bayar, and quickly. To save face, but people would still know. They always do. And could I marry Bayar? Could I take him home? To people that viewed him as a barbarian? And if I couldn't take him home, could I stay here? My family would never visit.

I didn't even really know Bayar. I've heard that people feel like that when they're getting married.

I thought through every scenario, again and again, as I sat alone in the small room, my hands pressed down on a thin, rigid sheet of sanitary paper. I looked down at my stomach. I looked pregnant. My stomach was larger and rounder. But that was impossible. Even if I was pregnant it would only be a few weeks.

And if I wasn't pregnant, I'd have to end it. I couldn't keep risking it. I'd view this as a warning from God. It was a warning from God. I understood. I had to stop and repent.

My legs hung down and my knees shook as I waited for the doctor and thought of all the stories of missionary women on foreign fields being examined by foreign doctors. A history of silent abuse. And I was alone.

I imagined what I would do if I was uncomfortable. If the doctor touched more than he should. If his hands moved up my thighs. But, what if he says he needs to? For medical purposes? What if he forces himself on me? What if I can't push him away? What if he's stronger? And what if I scream and no one comes? And who would believe the white foreigner over the local doctor?

My breathing became shallow as I waited. The door handle turned and my heart stopped. A Mongolian woman entered the room and introduced herself as my doctor. I sighed.

Her tone, her steady hands, and her perceptiveness slowly put me at ease. She told me before any results had come back that there was very little chance I was pregnant. She said she had an eye for it, and I didn't have the look. That my stomach didn't have the proper shape, and I was imagining things.

I'm not going to tell anyone. Either way. I can hide it, I thought.

After various examinations, the doctor left me alone. When she came back, she told me I was carrying. And it was growing in me.

***

"Is Lydia pregnant?" Alison asked her mother. Somehow, they had missed me joining them in the Mexican restaurant's bathroom. The mariachi music must have drowned out my footsteps, and the Febreze clouded their senses, and the lack of mirrors above the sinks left them completely unaware as I closed the stall door and took a seat on one of the toilets. "She looks at least five months pregnant," Alison continued.

"She didn't drink either," my aunt added.

"But that could just be her being her normal prudish self."

"She had to get pregnant over there," my aunt said.

"By one of them," Alison added. "Jeremy said she's been getting texts from someone."

"The father?"

"Who else? She never had a social life here. Never any guys at least."

"This is what happens when you preach abstinence."

"So much for Ms. Goodie-goodie. Do her parents know?"

"How could my sister miss it?"

"Has anyone talked to her about it?"

"Should we?"

I couldn't see them. But I could picture Alison smiling. Seeing me fail had always pleased her in some way. Life was a competition for Alison, and it was obvious now, she was winning.

I picked my feet up and placed them quietly on the edge of the toilet. When they left, I cried quietly, and waited long enough that they would believe I had left the restaurant.

***

At my next appointment, just a week before my grandmother's death. My doctor told me it was growing rapidly. It was nearly the size of a baseball and that at the current rate it would double in size within a month. She told me they needed to do surgery as soon as possible. She said I had to make a decision and she recommended that I go back to the States for it because they would be able to treat it better, and I would have a much better chance of recovery. But if they were to do it in Mongolia, there was a lot more risk. She explained that I'd never be able to have kids. She said I would need a complete hysterectomy to stop the spread of the cancer.

**

My phone buzzed while sitting on the toilet. Sent from Bayar at six in the morning, it reached me at six in the evening. This time in Mongolian, saying he couldn't wait for me to return.

I didn't tell him about the cancer. I didn't tell anyone. I told the doctor I wasn't going to return to the States. That I would trust the Mongolian doctors.

Bayar had been getting suspicious. But he seemed happy, and I caught him looking at my stomach from time to time.

After the funeral and the family meal, back at my parents' house, my mom asked why I seemed so tired. She told me what my cousins and my aunt thought.

"They think you're pregnant, Lydia," she said. "Are they right?" She fought back a smile.

I was speechless. Not because of the question, but because I could tell that the idea made her happy. Not like it made Alison happy, not spitefully. But there was hope in the smile, hope that it was true and there was a child.

My mom and I were never close. Now, we barely talked. She would send me an e-mail every few months, where she would tell me about our family and brag about my cousins. She would tell me about her job at the school, and how she wished I still worked across the hall from her. She told me how 'her kids', as she called them, dreamed of making something with their lives. They wanted to be doctors, and writers, and scientists, and that I still had a chance to do something 'significant' with my life. She had connections at the high school, and she told me she was sure she could get me my job back, if only I was willing to come home. She was angry at me for moving so far away. For taking her only chance at grandkids halfway around the world. She was fine with it at first. Until the day I told her I wouldn't ever be coming back. That I intended to do missions in Mongolia for the rest of my life.

"Are they right?" she repeated. Now, my mom bit her lower lip and her eyes watered as she waited for me to answer. Hope of having me back at home, hope of having another child, hope of my life changing direction and bringing me back to her hinging on my answer.

"I'm not coming home, mom," I told her. "I'm staying in Mongolia."

She smiled, reacting before the words registered. She looked away and said, "No." The smile faded. "You can't raise a kid over there—"

"I'm going back," I said. "It's my home now." I was shaking and on the verge of tears, as she left our living room and yelled for my dad.

***

Jeremy stopped by my parents' house the day before I was to return to Mongolia. "I brought you something," he said, reaching into his pocket and pulling out a plastic bag with three different bottles, and a piece of paper folded inside. "This is a natural solution. To your problem," he said. "There's some literature, a little brochure if you don't believe me. Totally natural. I had a friend who says it worked great. Get this, she said these mushrooms actually worked better than any prescription she was ever given. Natural is the way to go. The Japanese have been using it for decades."

When he left, I went to throw out the bag of mushrooms, the mushrooms meant to kill a baby that never existed. It struck me though, that when no baby shows up, Jeremy will believe his mushrooms worked. I took the brochure out of the bag before dropping it into the bin. It read *Polysaccharide Krestin: mushroom extract that fights cancer.*

Eastern Princess

My parents bought me new Nike sneakers for my fifteenth birthday, shipped from the states; they were black to hide Mongolian dirt. After three months of wear and travel in the Steppe, the silver Nike symbol on the left shoe was peeling off.

The night before we left Oyunchimeg's village, she told me that she fed her father to stray dogs. She took me to where he died and showed me the pile of rocks that marked his grave. Blue ribbons floated in the air, pinned between the stones. "This", she told me, "is where my father's chewed bones rot."

I misunderstood her. I must have. I wanted to ask why she did it, but I kept quiet and hoped she'd tell me. I had lied all week about how much Mongolian I knew, and she still believed I barely understood any. I could tell she still bought my lie by the way she used hand motions to communicate what she really wanted me to know.

Over the last five years, my family had developed a technique. During the summer, we would move from village to village, stay for a few weeks, make connections, and preach. Before we left, we would show a film. For some Mongolians, this was the first time they'd ever seen a film. We'd attract the whole village with a projector and set up the screen in the village's largest *ger*. Without an audio system for the projector, my dad narrated the projection. Our translator repeated my dad's narrations to the crowd, yelling over the clipping of the diesel power generator just outside the *ger*. When the film would end, the Mongolians would cry and shout questions. I can't imagine what it was like for the Mongolians to watch the film. They had no concept of Jesus, Israel, crucifixion, or even the Roman empire. My parents often had to explain that it wasn't a real recording, but rather a depiction of true events.

Oyunchimeg had led me out of the packed *ger*, taking my hand and waving me forward. I was happy enough to leave because the Mongolian summers are nearly as hot as the winters are cold, and the mass of bodies in the *ger* had me sweating through my shirt, the cotton clinging like fly tape to my back. And I was sick of the film. I knew my dad's script and moved my lips with his narration.

We walked to her father's grave, a mile or two outside of the village, but I wasn't worried about being missed —

the Jesus film was over four hours long, and my parents wouldn't notice I had left. This was their moment.

Oyunchimeg had brought her dog along, Bor Baavgai. The name meant 'brown bear,' and it fit him perfectly. From a distance, the mass of fur could easily be mistaken for a bear. Long haired, huge, and lumbering, the dog was miserable in the heat, his tongue flopping out the side of his mouth, dripping saliva onto the cracked earth. The village streets were mostly empty, save for a few kids who couldn't fit into the *ger*. They waited for their parents and supper, passing time by playing soccer.

Mongolian villages fill the space between the city, Ulaanbaatar, and the nomadic Mongolians of the steppe. The villagers live in *gers* like the nomads, but they are held in place, not by concrete like in the city, but instead, by wooden fences. Family units live together, a *ger* or two and an outhouse, hidden away in the tall fencing, their neighbor's similarly unseen.

This village was different than the others we had visited in the summers prior. It was strange, even for Mongolia. It was like arriving on another planet. There were holes in the ground, the size of golf balls, and there wasn't a meter without one. And dashing, diving, hopping from hole to hole were tiny mice with arched, kangaroo legs and rabbit ears larger than their bodies. The dozens of cats in the village, fat and lazy, never went hungry.

She told me it had been another night when her father had had too much to drink. "Vodka," she said. He beat her mother and continued even after she had passed out. Oyunchimeg tried to stop him. She hit him over the head with a sheep prod, but it only enraged him further. He chased her out of their *ger* and out of the village. It was late and dark, so there was no one to see her fleeing.

If I hadn't understood her, I might have thought she was reciting poetry or praying to some spirit, the way she spoke rhythmically, not looking at me, but instead watching the sun as it set. On the flat horizon, the jumping mice - millions of them - made the ground shimmer, vibrating all together, the light reflecting off their backs like water. There were waves and ripples. The ground was alive and shaking.

Her father had fallen, vomited, and choked, rolling on his back, groaning. "He was dying," she said. "On his own sickness."

I guess she wanted to confess because it felt good. How long had she been holding this secret? Even if she thought I couldn't understand, maybe she was unburdening herself. I imagine that when thoughts are concealed, they have a different kind of power. They fester and grow. But this wasn't really a confession because Oyunchimeg hadn't done anything wrong. I had misunderstood her. She hadn't participated in her father's death; she had let him die.

Then, Oyunchimeg explained how she wrapped her scarf around his neck and stopped him from catching his breath. "His eyes were blank," she said. "I could not leave him that way; he would smell and be found. I led the stray dogs to where his body had stiffened. The sun had started to rise, and flies were already on his eyes. I cut him open, a little, to get the dogs to taste him, and eat. Only Bor Baavgai did not eat." She scratched her dog behind his ears until he sat down and tilted his head up at her. "I told my mom he drank too much and must have died looking for home. And the strays found his body before I did."

She reached for my hand, and I stepped back. I used to not let any Mongolian girl touch me. It wasn't anything against girls, it was just that I had seen Mongolian girls the same as Mongolian boys: rough, dirty, only good for playing sports. And in the winter, wrapped in so many layers, I rarely could tell the two genders apart.

This summer, I began to notice how different the Mongolian girls actually were. Their faces were softer and slenderer than the boys. Their eyes were dark and deep, and I found myself trying to catch their gaze and hold it as long as I could before my stomach would lurch and my face would flush, and I'd be forced to look away. In the heat of summer, girls shed their layers and my chest would tighten as they walked by. Their perception of me changed too. They had largely ignored me for years or treated me like any other white foreigner. Now, they gave me special attention, and like Oyunchimeg, some sought me out and maneuvered to be near me.

It was Oyunchimeg's mom who had given my familya place to stay for the last week. Her parents, Oyunchimeg's grandparents, passed away a few years prior, and they used the vacant *ger* as a guest house for travelers. It only had two beds, so my parents got one, our translator the other, and I was given a cot. The outhouse had a stool with a seat, an upgrade from the last village, which only had a gap between two planks.

Oyunchimeg smiled the first time she saw me, holding my gaze until I broke and looked down at my feet, the Nike swoosh on my left shoe nearly all the way off, hanging on by a thread or two. She was younger than me, maybe a year or so, but she was just as tall, slender with shoulder-length hair. She wore a tattered red Bayern Munich football jersey — it was obvious from how tightly it fit her chest that it was meant for a boy. When I looked back up, she was still staring, still smiling.

From the first day, I had pretended to understand only some of what she said. I didn't want to deal with carrying on a conversation. I liked that we could be together without talking. It felt less awkward. I told her my name was "Oktai", a Mongolian name I had adopted for the summer. It was easier than having the Mongolians struggle to pronounce my English name. She told me "Oktai" was a funny name for someone who knew so little Mongolian. She said, "It means, he who understands."

I helped with Oyunchimeg's chores. We'd wash clothes in a slow-moving, frigid river. We'd skin the marmots, rabbits, and foxes that the men in the town hunted. At first, the other men and boys thought it was strange I stayed with her and didn't go out with them, but Oyunchimeg told them she needed the help, and they seemed content to let me do the work. We'd feed the gutted innards to the stray dogs. They were fond of Oyunchimeg and a half-dozen of them kept by her side in the village, but Bor Baavgai was the only one allowed to sleep inside the family fence. She always gave the brown bear the first and best bits of guts. He was bigger, stronger, better fed than the other dogs; the others patiently waited until he was finished before fighting over what was left.

My family had only been in the village for two days when she kissed me. I didn't even know Mongolians kissed. I had never thought about it because I had never seen anyone kiss. It wasn't a romantic moment, there wasn't even eye-contact before it, so I didn't have time to think about it coming, it just happened as the stray dogs snapped and growled over a juicy fox brain. She pinched my chin and kissed me. She tasted like *suutei tsai*, salty goat's milk. I hated the taste, but over the week, it grew on me.

"Uh, bayarlalaa," I said, the closest thing in Mongolian I knew to "thank you," my cheeks burning as she moved away.

Oyunchimeg laughed and continued removing fur from flesh.

She wasn't the first girl I had kissed, but she was the first Mongolian girl. My first kiss had been with another American. A family friend living in the country. A missionary girl just a few years older than me. What had started as a friendship from a young age changed. As with Oyunchimeg, Maggie had initiated the romance. She wrote me long notes, lengthy passages talking about God's love. She told me her dreams and desire to have a love with a man that mimicked Jesus' love for the church. I never responded to the letters, but the letters continued arriving for months until, during one of our parents' mission meetings, she took me to her room. Her brother Peter was back in the states, so we were often left alone. As our parents prayed in the other room, we pried each other's clothes off.

We never went too far. Or what Maggie said was too far. However, every time we met, we moved closer together. The next day, I would receive another letter. Telling me the night before was our last time and she had guilt because we had gone too far, and needed to pray about our relationship. If we loved each other, which she assured me we did, we could wait for each other. But, we continued. A knock on her bedroom door, a clang against the lock, and a frantic search for our shirts ended the whole affair, though the letters continued.

After Oyunchimeg's first kiss, they became a regular occurrence. I couldn't predict them, and wasn't brave enough to initiate them. I only knew they came when we were alone. I caught Oyunchimeg more than once checking after a kiss to see if anyone had seen. I wondered what she was looking for. Unlike Maggie, Oyunchumeg didn't have a father lurking in the other room.

When our parents found out about Maggie and me, her father took me out to breakfast. He bought us pancakes and coffee, which we never touched. As I reached for my fork, he asked what my intentions were with his daughter. I didn't have an answer because I had no intentions. It was Maggie with all the intentions. He asked what we did in the room and how long it had been going on, his face burning red as he asked how far we had gone. I insisted we only kissed as I looked at the entrance and thought about running. He lectured me about the importance of respecting a woman and keeping her reputation "beyond reproach." My parents had already given me this talk, but they also threatened boarding school. And I had to laugh at them because I knew they couldn't afford it or else I would have already been there.

Oyunchimeg's kisses with me were becoming more natural, less stiff, less like a high-five and more like a handshake, interlocking. I was familiar with her lips and became intrigued by the rest of her body in a way I never was with Maggie's body, maybe because Oyunchimeg's body was so different. Maggie was beautiful, but nothing about it interested me like Oyunchimeg's did. And it wasn't her breasts or her butt, or anything that other teenage boys talk about, gawk at, or whistle at — I couldn't imagine talking crassly about Oyunchimeg, because somewhere in eastern Mongolia, there was this perfect girl, maybe not perfect, but perfect to me. The words in Maggie's letters came back to me as I lay in bed, one *ger* away from where Oyunchimeg slept. I understood the letters now. They fit Oyunchimeg and me as they had never fit Maggie and me. Maggie said God had designed us to fit each other. That our desire for each other was holy and a reflection of God's divine love.

Oyunchimeg and I were different than Maggie and me. We weren't behind closed doors or communicating feelings in private letters; we were out in the open, under clear skies and bright stars.

I was fascinated with her arms. They were fit. Her biceps were smaller than mine, but defined, indented at the base above her triceps. There wasn't anything wasted: no extra skin, no imperfections, arms that were the way arms were *supposed* to be. Her legs were the right length, the right shape. She was quick and could outrun me, even without shoes. She didn't own any. I thought about giving her my new Nikes, but they weren't good enough for her, not saturated with Mongolian dirt or with a Nike symbol falling off. Oyunchimeg didn't need — didn't deserve — something broken.

Standing next to her father's grave, thinking about how she strangled her choking, drunk, and abusive father. Her arms looked stronger, too strong. Her toenails were dark and cracked. I noticed how Gobi sandstorms had marked her skin, leaving a series of blisters climbing from her toes all the way up her legs. I couldn't meet her eyes, so I looked above them, to where she had a tuft of hair between her eyebrows, right in the middle.

"Oktai," she said, as reached for my arm, but I pulled away again. It was instinctive. "Oktai," she repeated. "What's wrong?"

I stood up and pointed to the swell of mice - it was the closest Mongolia came to an ocean - and said, "Wow!" I hoped the English expression would sidetrack her, make her think I didn't know what she was saying, what she had said.

From far away, the mice were beautiful, they shimmered and shined, and made for the most incredible sunset I'd ever seen. But I imagined being among the rodents, their furry little bodies brushing against my legs as I breathed in their musk.

I was glad I was far away. I wanted to be far away. I wanted to be farther away from Oyunchimeg. I wanted to forget about the hair between her eyebrows, the marks on her legs, and her cracked nails. I wanted to forget the story about her father, to believe it wasn't true.

Oyunchimeg smiled and laughed, reaching for me again, thinking I was playing a game. She leaned in for a kiss. But I moved farther back, away from her and the pile of stones.

"Oktai?" she asked. But that wasn't my name.

I turned and ran down the hill. Mice bounced and hit my heels as Bor Baavgai barked, and Oyunchimeg called, "Oktai!" She yelled again, this time her voice cracking, "Ok-tai!"

I nearly tripped as I made it down the hill. I stepped on one of the mice, and it squeaked and continued squeaking as it hopped in a circle, one of its legs bent backward, crushed by my weight. Other mice continued jumping past it, leaving it sprawling until it came to a sudden stop. It lay on the ground with its small chest rising and falling, its large ears twitching, its blank black eyes looking up at me, its long hairless tail fluttering up and crashing down. It didn't make any more noise as I bent over it, still panting from the run. Oyunchimeg was coming down the hill, Bor Baavgai close behind her.

The last of the sun's direct light reflected off the Nike swooshes on my shoes. I pinched the bent swoosh and ripped it off. I felt better without it, freer, not worried about it coming off, or how it would look. The left shoe looked fine without it. It was only next to the other shoe that it even looked like it was missing anything. The shoes were perfect when I got them, and now they weren't. The mouse was fine before I ran away, and now it wasn't. Oyunchimeg was perfect when I first saw her, and now she wasn't.

Everything I had done only made everything worse., but Oyunchimeg hadn't changed. She had the marks on her legs then and the hair between her eyebrows and she had already killed her father, even if I hadn't known. I had changed was happier not knowing.

I raised my foot over the mouse and closed my eyes, thinking about how I had to kill it. Or forget that it was dying, but I couldn't forget. I stomped down and felt its small bones collapse.

I dropped the swoosh and turned back to Oyunchimeg as she made it to the bottom of the hill. I took her hands and without saying anything kissed her.

"Why?" she asked.

"I'm sorry," I said in Mongolian. "I can understand you."

She didn't answer, but looked back up at the stack of stones, silhouetted against the dark orange sky.

"I won't tell anyone," I said. "I understand why you did it, too. You had to."

She didn't turn back.

"I can forget," I said. "I can forget all of it. And I'm leaving tomorrow, you can forget me."

Oyunchimeg walked away, up the hill, Bor Baavgai by her side. I followed her, but she ran and disappeared as it grew dark. I followed the lights back to the village and waited for her, but she never returned.

In the morning my parents packed up our things and told Oyunchimeg's mom what a gracious host she had been. They thanked her for having her daughter keep me occupied. The village gathered and waved as we left.

The mice slept in the morning. The earth was still.

Wild East

"It's the difference between tipping over in a giant metal box and falling thousands of feet from the sky in a giant metal box," Matt said. He was trying to convince me it was safer than flying, that even though derailments do happen, they are less likely to be fatal, especially compared to airplane accidents. "Trains don't go up and down. The track is flat, and they stay on the path."

We had a twenty-minute tourist stop at the Great Wall. I took off my wedding ring and slipped it inside my coat pocket. Women pulled on me, muttering in Chinese, and pointing to my shoes. "Sorry, I don't speak Chinese," I told them. They laughed and left me alone, but only after admiring my coat, tugging on the sleeves, and repeating the English phrase, "Very good."

It had been almost two years since I'd had an incident; I hadn't had a single one since I'd met Matt.

We had only stayed in Beijing a few days, but already I was getting used to being mistaken as a local. I'd only ever been to China once as a child, on a family trip with my grandmother. I can barely remember it. The memories that stuck, were smells and colors — dark reds and green teas, and spicy, garlic street food that overwhelmed my American senses. These things hadn't changed. Even outside of Beijing, just to the north, the polluted purple sky provided the backdrop to the Great Wall.

Matt stayed in our train suite while I took in the wall. "Go ahead," he said. "I've seen it before." He had two books, a stack of papers, and his laptop laid out on the small table. The "presidential" suite my husband's company had sprung for was the same as the economy — the only difference was half the number of beds. Instead of four slabs to sleep on, stacked like shelves, there were two. But like all the other cabins, we shared a narrow bathroom with our neighbors. The locks were broken, so I held the door closed, and said, "occupied," to our suite neighbor's angry voice, as they tried to open the door.

This was our first stop. We'd only been on the train for a couple hours, and the journey to Ulaanbaatar would take three days. I felt nervous about leaving the train by myself and tried to convince Matt to come, but he refused and asked if I'd be alright on my own, and I promised I would be, because I knew this would be the only chance I would have to see the wall.

The group of Chinese tourists stood at the base, looking up. From where we were, the wall could have been a round tower. The brick structure slithered and curved up the hill, reappearing on top of another hill far in the distance. We didn't have time to go up onto the wall. The conductor yelled at us in Chinese, and I kept my eyes on the crowd, trusting I could head back when they did. I felt their eyes not only on the wall but on me and my American outfit. Not being able to climb up, we did the next best thing: placed our hands on the ancient stones. I thought about how strange it was that we were all on a train to Mongolia, touching the wall made to keep the Mongolians out of China. A coarse brick cut my finger, and I left a red fingerprint on the wall. I placed the cut in my mouth and held it there, tasting blood and dirt as I followed the others back onto the train. When I was a child, I had learned to breathe in ways that made crowds more bearable, in through the nose and out through the mouth, nice and slowly — focusing on filling my lungs to capacity.

The train was moving again before I made it back to our cabin. I slipped my ring back on before entering the suite.

"How was it?" Matt asked without looking up from his work.

"It's cold out," I responded. I laid down on one of the hanging slabs called a bed, and closed my eyes, breathing. I put my earbuds in and turned on a collection of Edith Piaf songs. My phone was nearly dead, and I had no service. The outlets on the train didn't fit my power adapter, and the motion of the train made me queasy. That's why I took Dramamine as soon as we boarded, but it wasn't helping, and my head throbbed as the train shook.

"Wait till we get up north," he said, over the French lyrics. "The hills here block a lot of the cold. Up there the winds rush down from Siberia."

Matt was assigned to work in Mongolia for six months. His job was to oversee a film project, a documentary series about the progress of countries after the fall of the Soviet Union. He wasn't on the art side, but rather the financial and scheduling. It was his job to make sure the director and crew were doing the work and not living to excess; however, I was getting the feeling it wouldn't take much money to live to excess in Mongolia. Even in Beijing, I felt like a millionaire. Matt hadn't left the hotel, but I had explored the market across the street. It wasn't my best idea; I thought I might collapse. It was too much. Too many people. I found I could be invisible without my husband. Normally a calming presence, I was glad he didn't come as I watched white foreigners being barraged by shopkeepers. They largely ignored me, except for the occasional point and shout in Chinese.

At a jewelry kiosk in the market, a woman had grabbed my hand and looked at my ring, her flesh rubbing against mine, the sensation burning. I resisted the urge to hit her as she talked and talked and when I didn't answer, she laughed and switched to English, "This is very nice, very expensive, you have very wealthy husband. I'll show you good jewelry for wife of wealthy husband." I slipped my ring into my pocket and made it back to the hotel without another incident.

***

Someone knocked on our suite door and I jarred awake. The music had stopped, and my phone had died. The steward spoke to my husband and closed the door. "He says dinner is open in the dining car," my husband explained as I took out my earbuds. My husband spoke functional Chinese, and I knew none, despite my parents' best attempts.

I got up to go to the dining car, thinking I should try to eat something, but my husband didn't move. "I'll catch up with you," he said. "I want to get some more of this done."

I didn't answer. I left the suite and closed the door. I slipped my ring into my pocket and moved down the narrow left side of the train, down to the dining car. Passing through railcar to railcar terrified me. The passageway shook violently. The door sealed tight behind me, and the door to the next car moved left to right and up and down. I held the handle tight and tried to convince myself it was perfectly safe: I'd never heard of anyone dying crossing train cars before. I stretched across the gap, avoiding stepping on the connecting metal plank, and went into the next car. The door sealed behind me with a pop.

***

"You should come with me," Matt had explained. "It'll be an adventure, a second honeymoon." It had only been a little over a year since our wedding.

This was never part of the deal. His work had been in Boston. He convinced me I could take time off from my work, but I would have to take off the whole semester. I had worked for five years as an assistant English professor at a community college outside Boston. This trip meant giving up my chance for internal promotion, and hoping that, when we returned to the states. I'd find another school with better pay.

"What will I do there?"

"You can write," Matt said. "You're always saying you wish you had more time to write. Consider it a sabbatical."

***

As I passed down another corridor, and the train shook again, I braced myself.

"The trains are far safer than the planes," Matt said. "On our crew's survey trip, the plane had to loop around the Ulaanbaatar airport three times because the landing gear wouldn't come down." He laughed. Matt could take situations that terrified me and make them into a joke. "I've heard before that you're more likely to survive a car crash if you don't see it coming. Something about not having time to brace and get tense. So, it's better if your body stays limp. That way you're less likely to get injured. So, the whole time we're looping around, I'm trying to sleep, thinking, it's better for me if we crash."

I cried as I passed through the economy cars. Crying wasn't something I was used to. I rarely did it, except when there was real tragedy — my father's death while I was in high school, my first college boyfriend cheating on me — now, I'd been having fits. Tears welled up without warning or explanation. With it came dread and fear that was out of my control and awfully and desperately, inexplicably sad. It was a new kind of incident, sadness replacing fear.

I was still crying as I followed the other passengers through another rubber covered passageway and into the dining car.

The dining car had a miniature chandelier hanging from its low ceiling; passersby had to duck beneath it to reach the tables further in. The car shook, causing a chorus of clinking glass. I wondered who the train company was trying to impress with the garish display of faux luxury.

I sat at the only empty table and peered out the window, taking my gaze off the gold trimmed plates and decorated aluminum silverware. The sun was setting as the train passed out of hills covered in lush green forest and into a brown, flat, and arid landscape that stretched to the horizon.

"Do you mind?" a white woman asked as she took the seat opposite me.

I didn't answer, shocked by the English, the first time someone didn't address me in Chinese since I'd arrived in Asia.

"Where are you from?" she asked. "The states, I assume."

"How'd you know?" I wiped my eyes to rid myself of any remaining tears.

"A Chinese woman would never sit at table four." She tapped on the table marker with the number four, and said, "And you don't look Mongolian." She picked up the menu and peered at it. "You also seemed captivated by the view, and it's not much of one, so you must be a foreigner."

I felt the tears coming again, so I turned away to the window.

"Sorry," she said. "I'm being rude. My name is Hannah." She put the menu down and held out her hand, keeping it there until I looked back and took it. She pinched my palm as we shook. Her features were sharp, dignified, and dark — dark hair, dark eyes, and dark winter wear, all set against her snow-white skin. She was older than me by a bit, in her mid-thirties.

"I'm Anna," I said.

The woman laughed. "Hannah and Anna," she said. "This meeting is destiny." She smiled, looking at me like she was waiting for something before she spoke again. "I'm an anthropologist. I'm working on my doctoral thesis. Writing it on the Mongolian people, particularly on their perception of western culture, and how they've accepted and rejected aspects of the west since the fall of the Soviet Union," Hannah explained, grabbing the menu. "Always soup," she said, tossing the menu down. "I'm not a big fan of soup, it's just never quite filling. Plus, they serve it with tea, that's like soup with soup. We should try something different." She waved over the waiter, a small Chinese woman and pointed to something on the menu and held up two fingers. Hannah thanked her in English and Chinese. "So, what are you doing here? Traveling alone?"

"With my husband actually," I said. Her eyes moved to my ringless left hand as I covered it with my right. "He's an accountant of sorts. He's overseeing the finances of a film project."

"Fascinating," she said. "Truly. And what are you doing here?"

The waiter set down our steaming plates. Another waiter followed the first, flipping our small mugs and pouring tea into them. Hannah kept looking at me as the steam rose from our plates and cups. And something about the intensity of her stare, or maybe the steam, made my eyes water again, and I looked down at the plate of orange and red clumps of meat, lined with vegetables — eggplant, okra — and a round clump of rice in the center. "I'm keeping him company and working on some writing."

"You're a writer?" she asked. "There was a time I wanted to be a writer, but the pressure got to me. I was in college and wanted to be a novelist, but that white screen and the blinking cursor cracked me. I decided that I would write, but only about things that were real, that I could see and study. History and real people, none of the made-up stuff." She mixed her rice with her meat, and I did the same. "I bet you're a good writer though, aren't you? The quiet ones always are." She ate and waited for me to respond.

"To be honest," I said. "I don't know. I haven't written much. I'm an English professor."

"Ah, if you can't do, teach, right?" Her eyes finally left me. They moved to the window. "Look there," she said.

Outside, just a dozen or so yards from the train, was a herd of horses — brown, black, grey, and everywhere in between, moving in unison at a slow skip next to the train.

"Wild horses," she said. "Sometimes this feels like the only wild place left on earth. The wild, wild east. Not sure you could find somewhere less populated. Maybe Mars."

"How many times have you been here?" I asked. I lifted my cup of tea to my nose, letting the steam and earthy aroma ground me, occupy my senses and allow me to focus on our conversation.

"Oh god," she looked up and to the right, "three times this year, and five in total. I love Mongolia, and Ulaan-baatar. It feels like the last bit of civilization, right at the edge of the world. It's untamed and uncontrollable, harsh and beautiful."

The rest of dinner, Hannah talked about her research. She talked about how her graduate studies at Oxford had led her to research the cultural clash of the east and west. She discovered Mongolia and was instantly drawn to it because of the lack of knowledge and literature regarding it. She thought she could be the first to really study and write about this place and the cultural tug of war between the old communism, the new western influences, and the ancient Tibetan heritage. She told me what to expect when I arrived, how to avoid being ripped off by taxi drivers and con artists. "Never believe the stories about tents burning down and families lost," she told me. "It's always a scam." She explained to me about the types of food I had to look forward to, including the worst thing she ever tried and said I should avoid at all costs. "It's rock hard cheese, covered in sugar. You might as well stick a finger down your throat."

All the while she talked, I looked back to see if Matt would be joining us, but he never came. When we were finished, she asked if I would join her for breakfast in the morning. We agreed to meet at the same table at eight.

"How was dinner? Sorry I never came. Time just slipped by," Matt said when I returned to the suite. Without the light from the outside, the connecting corridors were completely dark, making the walk over the metal slab all the more frightening.

We slept on separate narrow beds. It was the first time we hadn't slept together since our wedding. I found the shake of the train oddly comforting, it reminded me of when I was a kid, how I used to close my eyes in bed and imagine jumping on a trampoline. It was always the same trampoline — large, with an outer blue ring, in my childhood home's backyard. The grass around it always so green and the sky so blue, and I would jump up and down until I could really feel it — the wind, and my stomach dropping — and that's how I would fall asleep, rising and floating.

In the middle of the night, we passed into Mongolia and I stirred awake as the train shook. I thought we were crashing as the whole cabin tilted. But Matt assured me we were fine.

"They're just switching us over. Moving us with a giant crane," he said. It was too dark to see the movement outside, so I stayed motionless in the bed. "We're moving onto the Mongolian tracks now," he said as we lurched and there was a loud thud followed by a series of clicks and whistles. A few minutes later someone banged on our cabin door. "Customs," Matt said. He opened the door and handed a Mongolian officer our passports. The officer waved a flashlight around our cabin and held it to my face as he looked at the passport. Then he nodded, stamped our documents, and banged on the next cabin's door.

***

Matt was still asleep when I left for breakfast, I thought about waking him up and inviting him to meet Hannah. But I didn't. I went alone. And when I got to the dining car, Hannah was waiting for me.

"No husband?" she asked.

"He's still sleeping," I said. I realized I never put my ring back on after last night's dinner. But not wearing it felt freeing, like taking socks off before bed.

"Customs is a racket, isn't it?" she said, "As soon as we left last night, I realized I forgot to warn you." She took a sip of her coffee and scowled. "You'll want to get used to this," she stuck her tongue out as she placed the cup down. "Instant coffee. I've never missed Starbucks more than my times in Mongolia. Instant coffee just isn't the same." She smiled. "What's your cafe drink of choice?"

"Venti soymilk latte with a double shot of espresso," I said, almost instinctively, blushing as she raised her eyebrows.

"Wow, are you sure you're going to survive here?" She laughed and my eyes watered again, and I felt like cursing, but instead, I said, "I don't know."

"Hey," Hannah reached across the table and placed her hand on mine, and it burned, so I jerked away. "I'm only joking," she said. "You're going to be fine."

I wiped my eyes and took a slow, deep breath. "I'm okay. I'm sorry. I've been, unstable, of late." The words came out before I could stop them, and I regretted them, because of the look of pity Hannah was giving me, or maybe it was fear. Some people hear "unstable" and feel fear. She looked into my eyes and my gaze darted to keep from meeting hers.

"The Gobi is the coldest desert in the world," she said, redirecting us both to the view. "It's not what people think of when they think desert. Dozens of people freeze to death out here every year. Imagine that, freezing to death in a desert."

"It looks like a dried-up mud puddle," I said.

Hannah laughed. "The world's largest dried-up mud puddle."

There was silence and it made me uncomfortable, and my body responded to it by panicking, that familiar dread growing inside of me. "If you made a mistake and you only realize once you've committed," I said, breaking the silence. "What do you do?"

"Is this ordering the oatmeal type of mistake?" she asked, lifting her spoon and with it, the pasty oats. "Or getting on a train to Mongolia type of mistake?"

The door to the dining car opened with a pop, and I turned to see Matt walking towards us. "There you are," he said, taking a seat next to me. He held out his hand across the table to Hannah. "Matt," he said.

She smiled. "Hannah."

I slid my hand into my pocket and put my ring back on. "Hannah is an anthropologist, working on her doctoral thesis," I said to Hannah's nods. "Her studies actually have a lot to do with your company's documentary."

"Is that so?"

"Mongolia's acceptance and resistance of western culture," Hannah said.

"Oh, interesting." Matt waved to the waiter and ordered in Chinese, and then said, "Our documentary series focuses more on the industrial and economic side of development after the Soviet fall. With a real focus on how capitalism is changing the former Soviet nations."

They started discussing Mongolia — the recent changes, the influx of new money, its history, its place on the world stage. Matt explained the coal industry, Mongolia's natural resources, how if they could afford to refine coal more efficiently and cheaply it would solve their pollution issues and in turn their growing health crises.

Hannah talked about Mongolia's own MTV generation — big screens in the city center played the network non-stop, and now South Korean pop stars are on all the cereal boxes, and American pop songs play over the radios. She told Matt how the young men seek opportunities abroad, but the women have a harder time leaving the country, obligations to their families keeping them home.

So, I sat quietly as I looked out at that bleak brown, cracked earth that never seemed to end. Going further into it, I felt that emptiness. That growing gap. I closed my eyes, breathed in through my nose and out through my mouth, thinking of the trampoline behind my house, with all that green grass, and the blue outer ring. I focused on the feel of the canvas mesh on my bare feet, the smell of spring, wet and cool, floral, and the heat of the sun, even warmer as I jumped up closer to it.

The train shook, the dishes clinking on the table. Matt cursed as he spilled coffee on his lap. And I opened my eyes, my stomach lurching.

"This section of the track is rough," Hannah said. "It's so remote out here, it's rarely, if ever, repaired. When we get closer, I'll show you where a train derailed last August. The broken cars are still there."

"They're just abandoned?" I asked.

"Easier and cheaper than getting the equipment out here to get them back on the track."

I excused myself from the table. "I'll be back. I need to use the restroom."

Hannah asked if I was alright, and I nodded. Matt continued cleaning himself off. So, I left the dining car moving back to the suite, passing through passageway after passageway.

As I laid down on my bed, I slipped off the ring and put in my headphones even though my phone was dead. I fell asleep as I imagined my trampoline and looking up at a clear, blue sky. And maybe that's why I wasn't scared — instead I was fine because I was already flying through the air — when the train shook, and I thought it derailed, and I imagined the car on its side. I was fine. I was simply looking up through the window at that same, beautiful blue sky above my trampoline.

***

I opened my eyes to the noise of Matt entering the suite.

"Are you alright?" he asked. He took a seat on the bed across from me. He bent forward, his hands together, giving me the "counselor" caring face that he wore whenever I had what he called 'issues'.

I didn't move, and neither did he. I stared up at the ceiling, pretending my phone hadn't died and music was still playing, and he said, "What's wrong, Anna?"

I sat up and my eyes watered, and I was out of control again. "I want to get off the train."

"Cabin fever?" Matt asked, laughing and taking my hands. Then more seriously, he said, "It's only another day and a half."

"I got on this train and I can't get off."

"It's only a day and a half." He squeezed my hands. "Where's your wedding ring?" he asked, flipping over my hand.

"Just put away," I said, "to keep it safe."

"It's not safer on your finger?" He asked. When I didn't answer, he wiped the tears from under my eyes with his sleeve. "Come on," he said. "Let's go back and talk with your friend. Get some food and some nasty coffee, and you'll feel much better." He lifted me out of the bed by my hands and led me out of the suite. I didn't fight him. I followed him through all of the rubber-covered passageways, except for the last one, the one right before the dining car.

I let go of his hands and let him get just far enough ahead of me that the door closed between us. He didn't come right back, I wondered if he even noticed I was gone. I could breathe again as I stood in the dark passageway, the train rattling. I wished it would derail.

Beneath me, just to the side of the metal slab bridging the gap, I noticed a small tear in the rubber, not larger than a finger, but it let in light from the outside. I bent down, and through it I could see the brown blur of the track rushing away under the train. I reached into my pocket and took out my wedding ring, and after one last look at it, I pushed it through the hole in the rubber and let it drop onto the tracks.

Pajero

Peter remembers his dad's voice over the sharp ring-ing. "It's going to be okay." His voice brought light into the dark. He repeated, "It's going to be okay," as stars appeared, and constellations formed. Peter could never make sense of them. He could still see the same patterns when he closed his eyes at night.

Maggie knew he had snuck out of the apartment. She told their dad and he followed him. He wasn't fast enough to save Peter's ear or to catch the boys that had taken it from him, but he was fast enough to find Peter before he bled out. His dad carried him the half mile back to their apartment.

When Peter woke up, he was in his room lying on his bed, his head thumping, a buzz distorting his mom's voice. "Hospitals are closed on Sundays," she said. "What were you thinking?" She left the room as Maggie entered.

"Let your brother rest," she said, but Maggie pushed past her and knelt by the bed.

She was crying and staring at the bandages on the side of his head. "Dad went looking for them. The ones who did this." She nodded at his ear.

Peter tried to respond but his throat was dry and couldn't produce any sound.

"I'll get you water." She stood to leave. "It's going to be okay," she said. She repeated it to herself as she closed the bedroom door. "It's going to be okay."

***

"Can Maggie come with me?" Peter asked when his parents told him he was going to be sent back to the States. A week had passed but the bandage was still over his ear and the ringing still inside his head.

"Just you," his dad said from across the room. His mom sat on the edge of his bed.

"You're going to wait until Maggie loses an ear?" Peter asked. He tried to sit up, to give his voice some power, but since losing his ear, he would get dizzy if he stood or sat up too quickly.

His dad's face turned red and he said, "This is your fault. If you screw it up with your grandparents, you'll be out of options." His dad chewed on the inside of his cheek, as he always did when he was angry. He watched Peter, daring him to speak again. When Peter didn't, he said, "Good, it's settled." He left the room.

Peter's mom stayed, sitting on the bed, and looking at the floor.

"Mom," Peter said; his eyes watered. He would never cry in front of his dad. But his mom was different. "Mom, please send Maggie. Or give me one more chance to stay."

His mom didn't look up from the floor but quietly left the room.

***

Peter's mom convinced his dad to see if things could be worked out. And a couple weeks later Peter, Maggie, and his parents took a trip with another missionary family to a *ger* camp a few hours outside the city. His parents spent their time with the other missionaries, and Peter was forced to babysit the other missionary couple's young son. He took him horseback riding and when Peter lost the boy out in the woods, and came back late at night without him, both families scolded him and panicked.

"That's it," his dad said, when he got back from looking for the boy in a starlit Mongolian countryside. "We can't fix this. You're intent on putting yourself and others in danger. You're going to get someone killed."

***

The boy was fine; his horse had found its way back, just like Peter had said it would. The horse navigating by the same constellations that brought Peter back. The boy arrived before the others out searching for him.

But Peter's parents sent him back to the States, to constellations Peter couldn't navigate.

***

Peter lost contact with Maggie. She had sent letters and emails, and Peter responded, telling her how his life was in the States — quiet, filled with chores and taking care of his grandparents — but, when he thought about his parents seeing what he wrote, he couldn't send it.

Though Peter was two years older than Maggie, they had ended up in the same grade, the result of two years of failing from Peter, and his parent's idea when he was young, that it would be easier to teach the siblings together rather than separately. He was about to start college, moving from Florida to Colorado, to the furthest school from Florida that would accept him. But he planned to spend his summers back with his mom's parents at their Florida retirement community, doing the same jobs he had throughout high school — cleaning pools and mowing lawns. He thought Maggie would be there this summer. But instead, Maggie moved out of Ulaanbaatar to teach English in Khuvsgul, a town on a lake, a twelve-hour drive north of the city. He couldn't contact her even if he wanted to. After she finished high school, she decided she wouldn't come back to the States.

Peter was determined to get her to return. His grandparents, in their age and failing memories, had become less than people, helpless without Peter or their nurses. If he failed to convince Maggie to come back, it could be the last time he'd see her for years. When he received an email from his parents asking him to come visit after his high school graduation, he accepted.

***

"I'm only here to see Maggie," Peter told his dad as they drove toward Khuvsgal. "I'm really not interested in talking," he said, but his dad continued.

"Your mom's been reading a book about father and son relationships," his dad said. "She was telling me how sons often challenge their fathers."

"I'm only here to see Maggie," Peter repeated.

"Pete," his dad said. Only his dad ever called him Pete, and only when he was trying to be serious or pretending to be sincere — his tone would shift, his voice would deepen, and he'd sit up straighter. "Pete, I know we had issues when you were growing up. Moving to a new country isn't easy, and I'm sure we could have done better."

"You sent me away." Peter kept his eyes on the road ahead and bit at the inside of his cheek. "You could have—"

"I don't want it to end like this. We can work through this," his dad said. The car shaking before he turned his attention back to the road.

Peter put his head to his window. He felt tears coming but sucked in air to stop them and he convinced himself he was angry, not sad; he was angry. He bit his cheek harder.

His dad took a deep breath to collect himself and said, "Your mom tells me you've picked a school. I'm proud of you. I'm proud you've stuck with school despite," he looked towards Peter's missing ear, "despite falling back."

Peter worried that he'd do something he'd regret. He didn't want to show his dad anything, even letting his anger show was somehow letting his dad win, reinforcing his dad's thought that he was the one with problems, he was the cause. He kept focused on getting to Khuvsgul and thought about convincing Maggie she deserved more than Mongolia had to offer.

"I tried to make it work," his dad said, his face was turning red. He was looking at Peter and not ahead of the car. Peter watched him in the passenger side wing mirror.

The Pajero hit a bump and Peter's head hit the window. "Shit," he said, "watch where you're driving."

His dad cleared his throat and said, "I want to take the blame for what happened to you. It wasn't safe, and I should have been more protective. I thought I was doing what was best for you and Maggie. And if I had listened—"

"No," Peter interrupted. His eyes were watering now, but only because of the pain. "It's not — you can't," he said. "You don't get to take anything back. You took me and Maggie away from everything we knew. Our friends, our family, everything."

After a moment where his dad didn't respond, Peter continued. "You could make it better. You could make Maggie leave like you should have done before. Make her go to college. She doesn't deserve to be stuck out here." Peter felt the hole where his ear should have been. "She's still okay."

The Pajero climbed a hill. Peter's father stepped on the gas to make it over the crest. But they were going too fast as the hill plateaued and one of the wheels fell into a rut. Peter's father turned sharply to adjust and the Pajero rolled. The back of Peter's head hit the headrest and his shoulder knocked against the door. He crumbled up against the roof and fell back onto the seat.

***

Peter woke up outside the Pajero looking at the sky. It was an unearthly, vivid blue. He couldn't remember ever seeing the Florida sky like this, so open and clear. A single cloud, the size of his thumb, floated right in front of his nose. He reached up to grab it, but it vanished behind his fist.

If he had passed out drunk with his friends, he knew there would be pictures of him. They'd have photo print-outs all around the school, taped to lockers, fairy wings photoshopped onto his back. It would say something like, "Mongolina." They'd color in his missing ear and make it pointed like an elf.

Peter tried to sit up, but he was too stiff, and his muscles wouldn't respond. He relaxed and let his body ease into the ground. He wondered if he had school or work to go to, maybe he was missing something important. His forehead spiked with pain as he tried to think about what to do. He breathed and closed his eyes. It was bright but cool, and the air was dry. The breeze made him shiver and his back muscles clench.

He groaned and rolled onto his side and faced the broken wing mirror. It was covered in light brown dust, a crack through its center. His nose nearly touched the blood splatter that had created a constellation of red spots. He wiped it clean with his thumb and made make out his face through orange smudges. Dark liquid crawled out of his hair and down his forehead. He could feel the warmth moving across his eyebrow and down his cheek.

He sat up, this time refusing to let the weight of his head hold him down. He wiped his eyes and took a second to focus. He was looking out at nothing. It wasn't a Florida nothing. It was a brown nothing with the rare green tufts of grass and hills like distant waves. He was back in Mongolia. The blood that leaked down his face was thickening and drying in the sunlight. Peter put his hands in the dirt and pushed himself off the ground; an earthy and metallic smell of his blood came. He took more slow breaths as he stumbled about.

Behind him was the upside-down SUV. It lay at the bottom of the hill, crushed to half its size like a trampled soda can. Peter moved over to it wondering if he had been the one driving. He touched his forehead gently and wondered what it hit. He moved around the passenger side. Clothes, food, glass, fishing poles, hooks and bait, and one of the doors formed a trail up the hill.

Peter was alone, hurt, and lost. It would be easy for him to panic, so he focused on one task at a time, and tried to put the pain out of his mind. He went to the driver's seat and looked in past the bent door. Peter had to lay on the ground to see inside, his chest and cheek pressing into the dirt.

In the driver's seat, Peter's dad hung upside down, his eyes closed, his seatbelt suspending him above the ground.

"Dad!" Peter yelled. He got up and tried to open the driver's side door, but it was bent and stuck. "Shit. Shit. Shit!"

He got back on the ground and slid on his back, through the window, scraping himself and tearing his shirt on broken glass. "Please, be alive," Peter said, putting his good ear to his dad's nose. He held his breath and tried to silence his thumping heart, listening for a sign that his dad was alive. His dad was breathing. He couldn't hear it, but he could feel shallow breaths.

He unbuckled the seatbelt and tried to let him down gently, but he still crumpled onto the car ceiling. Peter crawled out from under the car and pulled his dad through the window and away from the wreck. He looked for injuries. Small cuts covered his face, and his left leg was twisted, unnaturally. His dad's hair was covered in blood, some dried, but some still dripped over his ear and onto the dirt.

Peter ran up the hill and collected scattered clothes. He limped, his legs stiff and unsteady. Each movement felt like it worsened his injuries. He wondered if he had been shattered inside and it was just sometime before everything fell apart.

He brought back with the clothes and used them as a pillow to keep his dad's head off the ground. He knew he shouldn't move his head, but he also shouldn't be here with no help. He checked his pocket for his phone; the screen was cracked but he could still read the small white text in the corner telling him, 'No Service.'

Peter dragged the crumbled door over to his dad and leaned it over him, resting it on one of the SUV's front wheels to shield him from the sun. He collected a bag of bruised apples, and three water bottles from up the hill and set it next to his dad. He felt like he was floating above his body. All his pain was distant, a hum somewhere beneath him, as if it was someone else's.

"I'm going to look for help," Peter said. "I'll take one of the water bottles. I'll leave you the others and the apples. I don't know how long it will take, but I'll find help." Peter repeated, "I'll find help," as he moved to the top of the hill. "I'll find help."

There was nothing but dirt tire tracks, leading down the hill in both directions. He had to choose which direction to go, knowing either could be the wrong choice, that maybe both were wrong. It was possible to drive for hours, even days in Mongolia without seeing anyone.

He tried to remember where they were, where they were going, but looking down at the wreckage and his dad; he decided he didn't have time to wait. His dad might not last long enough. "We didn't bring any extra gas, he must have known there would be somewhere to get more up ahead," Peter said out loud. He went back down the hill, passing the wreck and his dad, and following the dirt tracks forward. He took one last look at the wreck before turning his back and starting to jog. The hum of pain grew to a roar, but he wanted to get away from the wreck as quickly as he could. His dad's face was stuck in his head, pale and expressionless, more peaceful than Peter could ever remember him looking.

***

When he couldn't jog, Peter sat down. He could feel his heart beating inside his skull. He thought through the things he knew — where he was, what had happened — so he could try to remember the things he didn't. When Peter felt like he could keep moving, he got off the ground and continued along the road.

***

Two camels moved over a hill in the distance, Peter followed the tire tracks, and the camels did too, continuing past him in the direction of the crash, their humps slouched.

Peter hadn't prayed since losing his ear. He'd been tempted to pray before a few important tests, when opening acceptance letters from colleges, when a plane had severe turbulence over Chicago, but he'd been able to resist each urge. But as he approached another hill, Peter whispered, "Please, let there be something." He directed it to the sky and whatever spirit, or spirits, might be listening.

Over the hill, the scenery was exactly the same. It could have been a mirror.

Peter collapsed onto the ground. He had managed to put all the pain he was in, and hide it away, ignore it, so he could continue on; however, more nothing, only hills in the distance brought the pain back. He no longer floated above his body, but now was in it, trapped. He lay on the ground and looked at the sky, his eyes watering as the first stars appeared, shining through an orange sky. He wanted to scream, but he couldn't make a noise. He closed his eyes and fell asleep. Sometime during the night, the cold woke him, and he curled up and groaned, shaking and seizing.

***

He remembered seeing the stars, close and familiar. He was shivering as he drank the rest of his water and pushed himself off the ground. He continued walking as the sun rose and the heat increased. His thirst made him forget his hunger, and he felt dizzy and struggled to stay standing. He focused on his feet, moving one after the other, along the tire tracks, the road he hoped would lead to something. Around midday, the tracks led up another hill. Peter climbed it slowly, the wind whipping and turning his sweat-soaked shirt cold. Peter's body shook and he hugged himself tight as he reached the crest.

He braced himself for more disappointment but this time there was a white dot, far to the right of the dirt path. Peter squinted, held his hand to his brow, and recognized the shape. "A *ger*."

He felt like he was jumping through time as he moved towards the *ger*, losing consciousness and reemerging from darkness closer to it, his feet willing him closer without his prompting, until finally, he was there.

***

It was by some miracle that the owner of this *ger* had a vehicle, a Russian built jeep that reminded Peter of something out of a WWII documentary. After being given water, Peter mimed the Pajero's crash along with the few Mongolian words he could remember to the owner of the jeep, an older long-bearded man. The man took him in his jeep and sped to a village. He couldn't tell how far they had gone. The darkness came and went, and constellations of light would form, and Peter would wake again. Outside this jeep, just like outside the Pajero before, the land was looping and repeating, rolling and crashing like an ocean.

***

They arrived at a village and the man found a doctor. He didn't have a white coat, only a stained brown shirt and ripped jeans. He couldn't have been much older than Peter.

They traded the jeep for a white van. Its seats had been removed from the back and replaced with a thin mattress. The doctor, together with two other men and owner of the jeep, piled into the van. Peter passed out, looking at the pattern of rust stains and holes in the roof of the van, as the doctor cleaned and bandaged Peter's head wound.

***

They pulled next to the wreckage. The two camels Peter had passed snacked on the apples next to his dad. The men shooed them away as they got out of the van.

The doctor bent over Peter's unconscious dad.

"Is he okay?" Peter asked.

The doctor yelled to the other men and they rushed over, lifting Peter's dad and carrying him into the van. They laid him on the mattress and the doctor followed him inside. Peter waited next to the wreck.

The owner of the jeep grabbed Peter's shoulder and gave him a thumbs up. He pointed to the wreckage. "Pajero," he said, pointing his thumb down.

The doctor came out of the van and talked to the others. Peter couldn't understand what he was saying, but the tone was low and serious. The jeep owner waved Peter closer and pushed him into the van. He took his own seat in the front and they started to drive, not back to the village, but back over the hill in the direction Peter and his dad had come from.

"Ulaanbaatar," one of the men told Peter. They were headed for the capital. Peter wanted to ask how far, but he couldn't be understood, and it wouldn't make them get there any faster.

His dad was on his back, his head propped up on a pile of rags. The doctor softly moved his dad's hair away from his forehead and showed Peter an injury on the side of his dad's head. Above his hairline was a deep gash; bleached white bone showed where the skin had been scraped clean and a jagged piece of metal had pierced his skull. Already queasy from the rough road, Peter fell forward and gagged, his empty stomach tightening and moving up his throat. The doctor handed him a bottle of water and motioned for him to drink. Peter thought about the darkness his dad was seeing, and what lights might be there.

"It's going to be okay," Peter said, squeezing his dad's hand.

The van shook and Peter felt hot and flushed, his limbs tingling.

The doctor grabbed Peter's hand and put it on his father's chest.

"What's wrong?" Peter asked.

Tarkhan shook his head. "Ukhsen."

He put his good ear to his father's chest. "It's going to be okay," he said. He hoped his voice could be heard through the darkness.

It was as if the van stayed motionless. But everything else kept moving. The sun set as they neared the capital and the constellations spun above them and all of Mongolia.

Locusts

As Spring comes and Mongolia warms, the wind grows and the dark fog, made of coal and smoke, that covers Ulaanbaatar in the winter, dissipates, and for a moment the Mongol blue sky peers down at the city. Gobi sand moves across plains, steppe, and finally, over and down the hills. Into Ulaanbaatar, it flushes through concrete corridors, seeps under doors, clanks against windows, lifts the edges of felt tents, clogs engines, and burns eyes. Animals huddle together, their backs to the wind and their faces buried in each other. Stray dogs run for cover under bushes and parked cars.

As the sand moves on, it leaves what is left behind trapped in the city along fences, walls, and district corners. Then a new storm, trailing just behind the sand, enters. It's heard before it's seen, thundering. The black cloud vibrates as it floods over the hills. Its fist opens and its fingers spread through the districts and down the streets. The Mongolians hide from the storm, and curse it, knowing it means death to their livestock.

This time Chinese foreigners in the city ran to meet it, out of their apartments and into the streets to collect it. They filled jars and plastic bags with the large-eyed, giant-headed, long-legged creatures. Their kids laughed as the bugs landed on their faces, and mothers bit off heads and put the bodies into their babies' mouths. The swarm darkened the sky, blocked the sun, and the air, space, and everything in between was filled with chaotic movement.

Gan watched the scene from a sewer hole. He held the lid open a crack and grabbed one of the locusts on the pavement. He held it upside down, its underside revealed, the dark green and brown lines, scaled eyes, transparent wings, oversized mouth, and twitching appendages. He ate it, the head and all, crushing the brittle skeleton and releasing the warm goo and bitter and salty taste onto his tongue.

He called down the hole, but his shouts only echoed back up to him. With no response, he climbed out and joined the others in the streets collecting the locusts.

***

"Maybe families are taking the other kids in," Zorig said last spring, as they collected locusts together. They knew that if they collected enough, they could eat well for weeks.

"We'd see them around the city," Gan told him. "They'd tell us what happened."

"Perhaps families outside the city, in the countryside." Locust legs dangled from the corners of Zorig's lips as he spoke. "I've heard of them taking kids to help care for their livestock. It's a good life."

"So many?" Gan used his thumb to stuff more of the bugs into an empty soda bottle. After a few days the locusts that remained would slow; they would stop moving completely. They lived longer by staying motionless. And in the bottle, they'd stay fresh. But for now, they vibrated the plastic with life.

Gan grabbed a locust and held it to Zorig. "What if something's snatching us up? Just like the locusts?"

"And eating kids?" Zorig laughed. "Maybe we'll get lucky and be next," he said, smiling with bug stained teeth. "I think I'd be tasty," he patted his stomach, "and filling."

***

Now, a year later, Gan was one of the few kids left in the sewers. One by one, they had all disappeared. Gan didn't know where they went, but he was sure they weren't in Ulaanbaatar anymore. He'd been all over the city and had never seen any of them.

After filling three two-liter bottles with locusts, the sun began to set, and Gan returned to the sewers to sleep on the pile of fabrics and plastic he had collected over the years. This winter had been colder, and this time there was no one to huddle against and fight the cold. In the morning, Gan left his filled bottles and took several emptier ones. It was harder to collect on the second day of the swarm. Most of the locusts had been trampled. The sidewalks and streets were paved in red and green with the flattened insects. Gan looked in less populated areas of the city, to streets with fewer cars, where the bugs congregated on piles of sand in the corners of buildings.

Gan stopped outside his old apartment building where he used to live with his father on the third floor. He looked over the playground and the swing set where he had spent hours with his friends before his father was sent to prison. The collapse of a staircase had been blamed on the architect, his father. Three men had died in the incident. His father was given a life prison sentence on the count of three murders. Gan used to visit the apartment daily, hoping that somehow his father would be released and returned home. However, even this place had never truly been Gan's home.

At the age of two Gan was given to his father as a gift. Gan's father's wife had died, and his father's cousin had given the youngest of his three boys, Gan, as a gift to his grieving cousin. Somewhere in the countryside were Gan's true parents, parents he never knew and would never meet. But he had been told they never wanted him; that his birth mother had gone insane and had been told by demons to drop him in a river. He disappeared under the freezing rapids and was found further downstream, on the shore, naked, half-frozen and half-dead. But a Lama had found him and woke him.

"A Lama saved you, and he blessed the gift," his father had told him. "My cousin wasn't wealthy enough to care for you anyway. Your disposal was a gift to us both."

Gan often wondered about his birth mother; what kind of spirit would make her drop her son into the water; what the demon told her about him; what words it had whispered. And he wondered how his life went from a curse to be trashed to a gift to be treasured.

As he got older, Gan stopped returning to the apartment. His presence had garnered suspicion and mothers chased him away, throwing stones at him to protect their children. Even now, older and larger, Gan feared being seen and made quick work of the locusts around his old home.

In the next district over, he found more locusts. The half circle created by the apartment buildings had funneled a swarm against the front doors. Another boy had beaten Gan to the spot and was collecting the insects in a small box, but as he put them in, they jumped out. The boy pushed the box to his chest, trying to keep them from escaping. Gan recognized the boy from the sewers, Tsendyin. They weren't close, but he was one of the few that were left.

Gan moved to help him, but stopped as two men came out of the apartment entrance. They carried a large glass jar with a metal cap and spoke to him. They helped Tsendyin move his locusts from the box into the jar, collecting more. Gan watched as they filled the large jar and sealed it. They pointed up at the building, and Tsendyin looked up. He was reluctant at first, but then followed them inside. The door closed.

Gan continued around the district collecting and returned a few hours later to the apartment Tsendyin had gone into. Gan went to the door and waited for Tsendyin, snacking on the locusts. But he didn't come out, and as the sun set, Gan thought maybe he had already left and had gone back to the sewer. So, Gan crossed the city to the sewer where Tsendyin spent his nights. However, he wasn't there; instead, he found an older man looking through his things, collecting bits of clothing and fabric from the pile.

"Stop," Gan said. "Those are Tsendyin's."

"It's dark. And he hasn't come back," the man said.

"They're still his." Gan ripped the stuff out of his hands and threw it back.

The man spit on the pile. "It's garbage anyway." He started to walk away. "If he didn't come back," the man said, "he's not coming back."

"What do you mean?" Gan asked.

"They don't come back." He turned to leave, but Gan grabbed his arm. "Stop," Gan said.

But the man pushed him off and knocked him to the ground. "Do you know where they go?"

"They're stolen."

"Why?"

He tapped his chest and left.

Gan picked through Tsendyin's things, trying to learn something about him from the pile of garbage. Most of the kids had something, something they had left behind, something they had hidden. Over the last year, Gan had started collecting, remembering each child from the items they left behind. Gan saved their items, in case they came back, and if they didn't come back — and not one had — still he kept them safe. He had collected a wooden horse, a rusted knife, a plastic jeweled purse, a ripped and tattered football jersey, a scratched car mirror, a baby doll, a felt sock that smelled of gasoline, a toy train engine, and a necklace with a broken chain. Gan imagined each item had a story and a reason they were treasured, why they were buried and hidden among their things — gifts from parents or siblings, treasured childhood toys that reminded them of warm beds and full stomachs. Gan didn't have a treasure. There was nothing left of his time before the sewers.

Beneath the pile of trash Tsendyin slept on, Gan found a photo wrapped in a plastic bag. The edges were torn, and water had warped the image, but Gan could recognize a young Tsendyin standing next to two other larger boys, each a little like Tsendyin, their nostrils wide and their ears long. He smiled as he looked at the picture and traced the shapes with his fingers.

He flipped it over. Words were written on the back, but Gan couldn't read. He yelled for the man, hoping he could read, but he was gone. Gan decided to wait for Tsendyin and ask him what the words meant. But as Tsendyin didn't return, Gan grew impatient. He put the photo in his pocket, grabbed one of his bottles of locusts, ran to the nearest manhole, and climbed out.

People on the street cursed at him as he ran back down the dark streets, past his old home, to the apartment where Tsendyin had been led. Gan tried to remember what the men had looked like as he waited outside the building. All he could remember is that they weren't Mongolian, they were foreigners. Gan had heard about foreigners bringing homeless kids into their apartments, feeding them, and telling them stories of foreign spirits and demons and their powers over the world.

He moved from hiding spot to hiding spot, trying to make sure no one would become suspicious of him and make him leave. Stray dogs came over to him, sniffed him, and begged for food. He gave them a few locusts from his bottle and told them to leave, kicking at them. Sometime in the early morning, when Gan started to fall asleep, he heard the apartment door close. He peered across the street to where a man jogged out of the apartment. He recognized him as one of the two foreign men. Tsendyin wasn't with him. Gan thought about following him but didn't want to risk missing Tsendyin leaving while he was gone. He stayed, and a short while later the man returned in a large Russian truck with a canvas covered back. He parked the truck next to the door and reentered the apartment. Gan moved across the dark pavement closer, as close as he was willing to risk, ducking behind a bench as the apartment door reopened and both men came out, struggling as they pushed a large wooden box on a dolly. Gan took shallow breaths and knelt close to the ground as the men scanned the apartments and then lifted the box into the back of the truck.

One of the men cursed as they pushed the box further into the covered back. The other man scolded the first in a foreign language.

They lifted the back latch, tied up the canvas, and got into the cabin. Gan looked up at the apartment building as the truck started. He wondered if maybe Tsendyin had already left. Maybe he was still in there, or he was wherever these men were heading.

The truck rolled forward, and Gan ran towards it, jumping onto the back and holding onto the canvas. He pushed his bottle of locusts through the cover, untied the rope as the truck moved, and climbed inside as it turned onto a lit street. He tied the ropes and sealed the canvas behind him.

Gan crawled into the dark, feeling the truck bed on his hands and knees until the truck suddenly stopped. He was tossed forward, and his head slammed into the wooden box.

***

When Gan , the sun was shining in sharp rays through holes in the canvas above. The air was stiff and hot, and a locust climbed on his face, rubbing its back legs against his nose. He sat up slowly, and the locust jumped to the truck bed. Gan felt nauseous. His throat was parched, his head pounded, and he wanted water, but he only had his bottle of locusts. He crawled to it and took out several bugs and chewed them slowly. He closed his eyes and let the snack settle his stomach.

He sat next to the wooden box. It felt cold, so Gan rested his head against the wood. He realized it was freezing, its coolness coming through the wood. He pushed himself up and struggled to balance as the truck bounced.

The top of the box was latched and tied shut. Gan tried to untie the knot, but it was too tight, and he couldn't pry it loose. He looked around for something to help open the box. He dug through piles of empty cardboard boxes and rolls of plastic wrapping until he found a glass bottle. He broke it on the truck bed, shattering it to pieces. He carefully took one of the glass shards and used it to cut at the rope. Slowly the rope frayed and as Gan got more impatient, he cut and pressed harder. The glass dug into his palm and blood dripped onto the truck bed. With a final swipe of the glass against the rope, it severed. Gan dropped the piece of glass and held his bloody hand in a fist as he unlatched the box and pushed the lid up.

The box was filled with ice. Gan dug, the blood from his hand mixing with the ice and turning it pink. He reached something solid just below the top layer and wrapped in plastic was Tsendyin. Gan recognized his shape, curled tight, his head and neck bent unnaturally to fit in the box. Tsendyin's skin was blue, and he seemed to have shrunk.

Gan dug more, moving the ice to the edges.

"Tsendyin," Gan whispered. He ripped and tore the plastic off his face, and touched him, recoiling at his wet and oily skin, beads of liquid resting on him like dew. He tried to lift him, but some of the ice had attached to the plastic around Tsendyin and made him too heavy. Gan twisted Tsendyin and faced his body upwards. He put his ear to his chest and listened for a heartbeat. It took time for Gan to tune everything else out and hear the thick thuds, his own or Tsendyin's he didn't know, but he hoped it wasn't his.

"You're a gift, Tsendyin," Gan said. "You're alive. You have to be alive." The truck came to a sudden halt and Gan fell back down, sliding back along the floor. He protected his head as he hit the cabin with a loud thud.

The cabin doors opened and closed as the two men exited the vehicle.

Gan jumped up and closed the box's lid and redid the latch, working to make it look like it had never been opened as the men came around the truck. As they started to untie the canvas, he hoped they wouldn't notice the red bloodstains on the wood and the rope. Gan pressed his back to the box and slid down as the canvas opened and the bright sunlight flooded in. He closed his eyes as the men exchanged words and the canvas was closed again. Gan listened as the men undid their belts and liquid hit parched earth. Then the men got back into the cabin and the truck moved again.

Gan could escape now, before the truck was moving too fast, but now he could make it back to the capital. He would be safe, even if Tsendyin wasn't. He could warn what few kids were left about the ice box. He could tell them that demons had taken the children, demons with foreign tongues. That they snatched them up and took them far away. It could be too late for Tsendyin. But it wasn't too late for Gan. He moved away from the box and peeked out through the canvas. There wasn't a road. Behind them the truck kicked up dust, and through the brown haze, Gan saw sharp rock faces jutting from the edges of hills. But there were no people. No one to shout to for help. No one to signal. There was only Tsendyin frozen in the box. Gan felt in his pocket for the photo. He took it out and flipped it over to the words on the back. He moved his fingers along the letters.

Gan removed the lid again, digging the ice out of the box and into the truck bed. He knew if the men stopped again and looked, they'd know he was here, and he would end up in the box with Tsendyin. But he had made up his mind. They would both escape, and Tsendyin would tell him what the words said and what they meant. Gan pulled at the plastic and chipped away at the ice attached to Tsendyin's legs and pulled him out of the box and onto the truck bed. His body was stiff and held its huddled shape.

"Wake up, Tsendyin," Gan said. He slapped his face gently. "Please, wake up." The boy's body didn't move. Gan again placed his ear to his bare chest. If they were there, the thuds were fainter but quicker than before.

Gan dragged him to the back of the truck and untied the canvas. He opened it, tying the canvas to either side and letting the sun hit Tsendyin. He glistened in the light, the cold water running off him like sweat. The sky was bluer here. Gan had never seen it like this in the city. And there wasn't a cloud in sight. They seemed to be leaving the hills behind; the land smoothed and flattened. The earth behind them was cut in two by the trail the truck had made. Gan leaned out the back and looked in both directions. The flat nothing spread out in every direction, and Gan wondered where these men were taking them. Perhaps they were demons taking them out of the world, off the edge.

This was the farthest Gan had ever been from the city since he was a child, and he had no idea how far that had been. "My family could be from out here," he told Tsendyin.

The sun moved across the sky above them. Gan kept Tsendyin and the bottle of locusts in the light. The heat brought the locusts to life and the bottle shook, but Tsendyin stayed still, his body motionless. Gan didn't understand why the heat wouldn't wake him.

"They're going to stop again soon," Gan said. "I need you to wake up. We'll jump out of here. We'll find people. We'll work for them. Or we'll make it back to the city. We'll eat well and survive. You only need to wake up."

Gan collected ice, held some to his cut hand, and wrapped more in plastic. He left it in the sun and let the ice melt and drank from the pooled water. He thought about forcing Tsendyin to drink as well, but he worried about him choking. Gan snacked on his locusts. They flew and hopped; the bottle shook, Tsendyin was still limp.

The sun was getting low. Gan felt Tsendyin. His skin was moist and slick, and he was still cool. Gan took ice and held it to his own head as it throbbed. "Tsendyin, they will stop soon. The sun is setting, and they have been driving for hours."

The truck slowed and Gan feared it was too late to escape. He reached for the canvas but stopped as he looked down. The dirt on the ground had turned to small stones. The truck slowed more and lurched forward with a splash. Running water covered the stones and the back tires as they entered a river.

The water rose swiftly, nearly to the truck bed, and Gan wondered whether the water would flood in, or the truck would stop. But it pushed forward through the river.

"This is our chance," Gan said. He reached into the water and splashed it onto Tsendyin. The boy didn't move. He stood up, put his hands under Tsendyin's arms, and held his bottle of locusts in his armpit. Then he dragged him to the edge of the truck bed and fell back into the water, pulling Tsendyin with him. The water was swifter than Gan had expected. It pulled his legs from under him, and even in four feet of water Gan was dragged down. The locust bottle popped out of his arm and floated down the stream, but Gan refused to let go of Tsendyin. He tried to get their heads above the water, pushing off the river bottom, but the rocks under his feet gave way and he slipped. The river rolled and twisted him as it dragged him down. Gan hit the riverbed and lost Tsendyin.

Without Tsendyin he was able to get his own head above the water. He kicked repeatedly at the rocks below to keep himself up. Above the surface he could see the truck, now far behind, pulling out of the river and continuing forward. But Tsendyin wasn't anywhere. He was still somewhere under the water. Gan yelled for him, but his words were swallowed by the river.

He pushed off the ground and climbed to the edge of the water and watched for Tsendyin. He didn't resurface. Further down the river, the setting sun reflected off the bottle of locusts, and up and across the river the truck moved further and further away.

Gan climbed out of the river and ran downstream following the bottle of locusts. "You're a gift, Tsendyin!" he yelled. He yelled again between fits of coughing. He kept running and kept looking over the surface of the river. The truck disappeared into the distance and he was losing the bottle. The river flowed faster than he could run and grew deeper downstream. It got darker and the landscape turned orange. The river reflected the harsh light and Gan squinted as he searched for Tsendyin. Twice he reentered the river nearly drowning as he chased what turned out to be nothing but glare. The sun set and Gan moved out of the water and collapsed on the shore, shivering as the hot day turned into a cold night. Gan took the photo out of his pocket and unfolded it. "What does it say?" he asked. The words on the back of the photo had smeared even more, and the photo was splitting where it had been folded. Gan was losing all he had left of Tsendyin. "What does it say?" he yelled.

This time there was no one to save him, no Lama to guide him back into the world. He set the photo in the river and let it float away.

Gan laid down and watched the stars move above him, brighter and closer than he'd ever seen. He rolled over and curled into a ball, shaking. Two stars across the river moved together, their light growing brighter and closer.

"The truck," Gan said. "The demons." The truck lights turned and started along the riverbank, following the opposite shore towards him. He pushed himself off the ground and waded into the river. "Sorry, Tsendyin," he said as he got deeper. "Sorry, Zorig." He thought about the things each one left behind as he moved into the river. "Od, Chimeg, Yul, Tab, Suhk, Chinua, Otgun." He named more of the sewer kids as he lost sight of the stars, slipped under the water, and was taken away by the river.

Acknowledgments

Some of these stories first appeared in journals, magazines, or anthologies: "Soviet Skatepark" in Stories That Need to Be Told 2018 Anthology, "Mongol Boys" in Allegory Ridge's Archipelago Vol. 2, "Eastern Princess" in Running Wild's Anthology of Stories Volume 4, "Locusts" in Inverted Syntax's The Fissured Tongue Series.

A special thanks to my mentors, Gina Ochsner and Robert Clark, for pushing this work to be its best.

Jonan Pilet has called many places home — Ulaanbaatar, Chiang Mai, Seattle, Ohio, Pennsylvania, Upstate New York, and Oxford — and they all have a bit of his heart. Currently, he lives in Upstate New York. By day, he is a journalist, and by night, he is a novelist. He studied writing at Houghton College, the University of Oxford, and received his MFA at Seattle Pacific University. Pilet has had short stories published with Allegory Ridge, Funicular Magazine, Inverted Syntax, Open Minds Quarterly among others. On the weekends, he goes on hikes with his wife and their aging Siberian Husky, cheers on his Seattle Seahawks, and reads his expanding list of favorite authors. To keep updated with Jonan's work, follow him on Instagram or Twitter — @jonanpilet, or visit his website — www.jonanpilet.wixsite.com/author.